KITTY'S DEPUTY

A SILVERPINES COMPANION TALE

TONYA VANWINKLE

ACKNOWLEDGMENTS

To Jesus, the Master Storyteller and Ultimate Creator. Thank you for the gift of love, the gift of storytelling, and the desire to touch another's heart through the simple words I write. May they always be led by your hand.

To David, Ashlynn, and Brier, I love you so deeply I can never fully express it. You are my heart. Thank you for supporting me, inspiring me, and continuing to push me as I pursue my dream.

To the authors of the Silverpines series, thank you for the opportunity.

To you, the reader, thank you for taking the time to read my little story. I hope you enjoy it and I look forward to hearing from you.

May God bless you all.

FOR BRIER

"You are whoever you want to be...
You just have to decide to be it."
- Unknown

Not long ago I realized my babies are no longer babies. They have become busy, independent people in pursuit of their own lives. While I may wish for them to be little again, I know I'm blessed with each moment we have together, and I shall treasure them forever.

During the first steps into this new season of life, Brier said something that was profound: *"Well Mom, what did you want to do before you were Mom? Perhaps, it's time to do that, whatever it is."* He was slightly frustrated with me, but he helped me. I wish I could help him now. I see his frustration and I feel his worries. It's time for him to make some big choices, choices only he can make.

My plan for after high school was to escape, to get the heck out of there, and my ideas for that were all over the board. They were just the route that would take me out of town. The first was to join the Navy. The second was be a barrel racer and ride the rodeo circuit. The third was to be a counselor, but I had no idea how to pay for that and didn't believe in myself enough to pursue it. Then there was the idea that I held so close to my chest that few knew about it; to be an author. But who in their right mind would ever pay me to write a book?

God had many other plans for me, and while the Navy wasn't a part of my story, the military still was, but in the capacity of a military wife. Riding the rodeo circuit and traveling from place to place wasn't a part of my story either, although traveling the world was. Counseling students or working with social services wasn't a part of my story either, yet sharing my experiences and my testimony with others was. As for the writing, I never stopped, but I never allowed it to breathe. I never gave it life. Instead, I wrote my little stories, poems, sermons, and blogs in silence. I dreamed up idea after idea, tucking them all safely away where no one could tell me how much they sucked.

It took me thirty-eight years and a push from you to admit who I am. I know that, right now, the choices seem daunting and there are so many, but I also know it won't take you thirty-eight years to figure it out. My children are old souls, so son, you've got a head start. You are an intelligent, wise, and confident young man. I look forward to watching your story unfold, because whatever you decide, you'll do great. I love you, buddy.

Thank you for pushing me and for inspiring Milo's story with your caring heart, compassion for others, and strong sense of right and wrong.

Love,
        Mom

IN MEMORY OF

My Grandma

Dolly Elizabeth West

PROLOGUE

"Where is she!" Natalie O'Byrne screamed as she barged into the room, the door banging against the wall, startling Kitty awake.

"Where is who?" Kitty growled as she sat up, rubbing her eyes and trying to keep her Irish temper in check. It wouldn't do for Natalie to know the things she shouldn't, like where Abby was.

"You know of whom I speak. The servant girl that you have the audacity to call a sister. Where is she?" Natalie demanded.

"I assume she is still sleeping," Kitty responded through gritted teeth before yawning. "I have yet to see her this day." She glanced out the window, the sun was barely shining.

"Well, she is missing. I assure you she is," huffed Natalie, her hands on her hips as she spun about the room. The woman was maddening.

"Abby would not run off. What are you talking about? Did *you* do something to her?" Kitty asked, slipping a worried tone into her voice and praying it was convincing. She didn't have the acting skills Natalie had.

"I did nothing to her." Natalie stuck her nose in the air as she whirled around, making Kitty want to reach out and hold the woman in place by her shoulders. "I only went down to tell her of your father's passing and that I had arranged for her employment elsewhere." Natalie smiled, and Kitty longed to slap the grin from her face. How dare she! What right did she think she had?

"Why would you do that? This is her home." Kitty gripped the blankets in her hands.

"Well, it is no longer, and if you disobey me or help her in anyway, it will no longer be yours, either." She stormed out of the room, slamming the door in her wake.

Kitty sat shaking, her hands still clenched. She'd known this was coming. Her stepmother was one of the vilest creatures she'd ever met. She treated others like rubbish and it made Kitty's blood boil. She still could not believe how her father had ever fallen for that woman's charms. Thankfully, he'd realized what his new wife was before he became too ill to speak. Together they had concocted a plan, and Mrs. Natalie O'Byrne was in for a rude awakening.

For a moment, she let the small grin form across face. Her papa was a genius. Too bad his wife hadn't taken the time to notice, or better yet, good thing she hadn't. She released the blankets and threw them back, rising from her bed to pad toward the wash basin to scrub her face. She pulled out her simple black mourning dress and put it on, the dark color making her skin appear paler than normal. She had much to do this day, but if she rushed, Natalie would surely become suspicious of her. That was something she could not afford, she thought, as she tied her coppery locks back with a black ribbon. She needed to get to Abby and get her to safety, then carry out the rest of the plan. Keeping her temper in check was going to be her biggest obstacle, but Papa believed in her, and she could do this. She would do this for him, for Abby, and for herself.

Slowly, she descended the stairs and entered the dining room for breakfast, where she found Natalie sitting as if she were the Queen of England—and not wearing mourning clothes.

"Are you not even going to mourn my papa, your husband?" she demanded.

"Do not speak to me in such a manner. I am the lady of this house and I shall dress as I please. I am in deep mourning. I, however, do not see the point in wearing that drab garb,"—she pointed at Kitty—"until the funeral. Dark colors look atrocious on me." She sipped her tea, her pinky pointed perfectly in the air.

"I see," Kitty responded, saying nothing more as she spread strawberry jam on a slice of toast, unsure if she'd be able to stomach much more than that. She knew she needed to keep her energy up. She was just unsure how to do it at a time like this.

"I thought you might." Natalie grinned in a way that made Kitty's skin crawl.

"Do you want me to go and search for Abby? I can usually find her, but I don't think she's truly run off," Kitty said.

"For who?" Natalie's thin eyebrow raised with the question. Physically speaking, her stepmother was not exactly an ugly woman. She had blunt features, a pointed nose, and a chin that matched. Her lips were full, and she often painted them red, reminding Kitty of a saloon girl. Her hair was black as night with no sign of aging. Her large eyes were bright green and razor sharp. Perhaps some men found her eyes alluring, but Kitty thought they resembled that of a snake.

"My sister," growled Kitty, "You woke me to tell me she was missing, after all."

"Oh, the servant girl. No, I do not wish you to waste time on such frivolous matters," Natalie said waving off the question as if it didn't matter.

"I see," responded Kitty, realizing perhaps the fewer words she spoke the less chance she had of her temper exploding.

"I wish for you to go see Father Jacobs and make the arrangements. I am far too distraught to do so," claimed Natalie.

"I see." Kitty fought hard not to roll her eyes. Her stepmother didn't even have red rimmed eyes or tear stained cheeks. She looked far from distressed. How could she be so fake?

"Besides, I'm sure visitors will be stopping by to offer their condolences. It would not do for the lady of the house to be away at such a time, nor would it be expected of me."

Yet, you expect it of me, and he was my papa!

"I see."

I'm sure you will play the part of the grieving widow well. Say, I'm getting good at these short answers, Kitty thought while clenching her jaw. *Now, if I could just make my escape.*

"Shall I go now then?"

"Yes. Take the wagon, not the carriage." Natalie instructed with a look that left Kitty feeling slightly uneasy. Surely, she didn't know. They'd been ever so careful. Abby had left within minutes of papa's passing and gone straight to the hidey hole where they'd often played in their younger days.

Kitty calmly left the table and her half-eaten piece of toast. She grabbed her black shawl and headed out the door to the stable, all the while feeling as if bright green evil eyes were penetrating her back. Perhaps, that's why Natalie instructed she take the wagon, she wanted to be able to see *who* might be in the wagon with her.

"Morning, Miss Kitty. I'm sure sorry about your pa. You

need the carriage readied?" Bart Jones, their main stable hand, asked.

"Thank you, Bart, but no, I'll be taking the wagon today, per Mrs. O'Byrne's orders. I do think she's watching me," Kitty said.

"You be careful, Miss Kitty. She is a dangerous one."

"That she is, Bart. Did you accomplish the task I asked of you?"

"Yes, Ma'am. Everything you required is waiting, and Mr. Allen is prepared for your arrival," Bart answered.

Kitty gathered her skirts and climbed up onto the wagon seat, taking the reins in her hands as she turned to Bart. "I'll return as quickly as I can. If a problem arises, you know who to send to warn me."

"Yes, Ma'am. We won't let no harm come to you or Miss Abby."

"Thank you, Bart."

Kitty steered the wagon toward the hidey hole to fetch Abby...

Singing loudly, Kitty drove through the woods where their childhood Hidey Hole was. She thanked God that her stepmother knew nothing about it. No one but she and Abby knew of its existence. As she drew closer, her heart raced at the thought of this being her last moments with her sister. Taking a deep breath, she slowed the wagon to allow Abby to get on. Kitty looked around to make sure no one was watching. As soon as Abby was aboard, Kitty flicked the reins and prodded the horses toward town.

"I have a bag for you. I need you to look through it," Kitty said without looking at Abby.

"What's in it?" Abby questioned as she picked up the small bag at her feet.

Kitty watched as Abby silently dug through the handbag

and found the letters addressed to her. "Open Papa's letter first," Kitty said.

"But, Kitty, this is your handwriting."

"Papa was too weak to pen the letter." She choked back the sob that threatened to escape. "I–I'm sorry, Abby. I just miss him. I penned the words for him, but they are *his* words, not mine."

MY DEAREST ABBY,

If you're reading this, I have departed from this earth. I did not want to leave you or Kitty, but the Lord has been calling me home for some time now. I could not leave peacefully, however, without taking care of a few matters in order to protect my daughters and ensure their future. I did you both a great disservice in selecting your stepmother. I pray I do not make the same mistake in selecting your husbands. Do not be cross with Kitty, she did only as I instructed. Enclosed are your train tickets and two letters from Reverend Samuel Bates, your future husband. I wish I were able to walk you down the aisle, and that you were able to marry for love. I do pray you will find love within this arrangement, for love is one of God's greatest blessings. Go with God, Abby.

All My love,

Papa

KITTY CONTINUED to watch her sister through the corner of her eye as she drove the wagon into town. Tears streamed down Abby's face as she pulled out the next envelope and read it aloud.

DEAR POTENTIAL BRIDE,

I am Reverend Samuel Bates of Silverpines, Oregon. I am thirty-one years old, with blonde hair and green eyes.

Abby gasped, and her hands shook, rattling the letter. "It couldn't be helped Abby. Reverend Bates is the only advertisement Papa said suited you. I'm sure his green eyes will be beautiful and not so frightening as the ones we're used to seeing. Have faith and trust."

Kitty wished she knew a way to remove Abby's fear, but Natalie O'Byrne had the type of green eyes that haunted you in your sleep and long into daybreak. No matter how hard Kitty had tried to protect Abby, she couldn't shield her from all the pain and sorrow *that woman* had caused.

Abby took a deep, yet shaky breath then continued reading.

I long for a helpmate with whom I can share my life and work. I am looking for a strong Christian bride with a compassionate and gentle soul, between the ages of eighteen and twenty-six. I would be well pleased if she enjoys baking cookies and taking long walks. If this sounds like you, I look forward to your response.

Sincerely,

Reverend Samuel Bates

"There's one more letter in there, well it's more of a short note," Kitty said softly.

Dear Abigail,

Thank you for accepting my proposal. Enclosed is your train ticket to Silverpines, Oregon. I anxiously await your arrival and will meet you at the train depot on April twenty-third.

Your Husband-to-be,

Samuel

* * *

"KATHLEEN O'BYRNE! You answered this man's ad pretending

to be me?" Abby asked, the color draining from her face, her eyes wide and overly bright.

"Please don't be angry. You only call me Kathleen when you're upset, and you know how much I detest it. I do understand why you would be upset, but Abby, this is the only way I can truly protect you right now. I didn't know what else to do when Papa suggested we marry," cried Kitty.

She hated that she had to send Abby away, but it truly was for her own safety. They'd known this day would come. They'd planned for it…well, *she* had planned for it. Abby had known there was a plan but not so much the details of it. Keeping the secrets from Abby had not been easy. It only seemed safer to keep things close to her chest. It wasn't that Abby couldn't keep a secret, it was just the fewer who knew of the plan, the better. Heaven forbid if someone had overheard her telling Abby; the plan would be ruined and Abby in grave danger.

"I'm not angry, Kitty," Abby replied softly as she reached for her sisters' hand. "I am in shock. We just lost Papa, the only home we've ever known, and now I'm getting married to a man I've never met. And he has green eyes. Green eyes scare me! I think I have a right to be a little upset, but I'm not angry with you," Abby said.

"Your train, it…it leaves today, Abby. This very afternoon." Kitty sobbed as the tears flowed freely down her face.

"It's okay, Kitty. I will do what I must, and you will be joining me soon, correct? Wait, you said Papa suggested *we* marry."

"Yes Abby, I too am going to Oregon to marry. I'll barely be a week behind you. I have to take care of things here and then I will be on my way." Kitty watched as Abby's eyes widened in shock.

"You are getting married? I thought you never wanted to marry?" Abby questioned.

"I don't, but I am. It is the only way I can remain close to you. I tried to find a set of brothers looking for brides, but Papa disagreed on each one I found." Kitty swiped away the tears and tried to give Abby a smile of encouragement.

"We will be okay then, as long as my groom truly accepts me when I arrive. Did you tell him of my heritage, of my mother?" Asked Abby.

"I did not, but he will accept you, Abby. You are beautiful and everything he asked for, down to the baking." Kitty smiled. She loved Abby's baking, she could own a bakery if she'd believe in herself just a little bit and stop fearing what everyone else thought of her. After a few negative experiences and hateful remarks, Abby rarely left Rosendale, content to remain at home away from the judgmental eyes of others.

"But, Kitty," Abby lowered her head in shame, "I'm tainted," she whispered.

"Abigail Jane O'Byrne! I never want to hear you say that again. You cannot go believing the vile things that evil woman has said to you. Do you hear me?"

"But Kitty, it's true. You know it is. Look at me. I'm not white like you. I'm different."

"Thank the good Lord above. You, my dear Abby, are simply not as pale skinned as I. You look as if you've been baking in the warm Georgia sunshine and that it has blessed you with a golden glow versus the red raw skin it bestows upon me. It's nothing more than that, Abby. Reverend Bates will fall head over heels the moment he lays eyes on you. You are not to worry and those words are not to be repeated," Kitty said, matter of fact, as she patted her sister's knee and drove the wagon toward Mr. Allen's office.

"Look Kitty, there's Mr. Allen, there," Abby said as she watched the man quickly approach them with a white rectangular box under his arm and an odd expression on his face.

"Miss O'Byrne and Miss O'Byrne, I'm glad to see you made it. I was beginning to worry. Were there any problems?" he asked.

"No sir. However, Stepmother is aware of Abby's absence. I do believe she was watching me as she instructed me to take the wagon instead of the carriage to Father Jacob's. She did mention this morning that she had found Abby *other* employment." Kitty rolled her eyes.

"That she did. I am sorry to say, Abby, we must get you safely stowed away onto that train immediately," Mr. Allen explained, as he shuffled uneasily, his feet kicking up dust that peppered his pressed gray trousers with brown specks.

"What employment did she find for me, sir?" Abby inquired.

Mr. Allen looked back and forth between Abby and Kitty, coughed once and then answered, "The word around the rumor mill, Miss O'Byrne, is that a Mr. Douglas Bloomberg, to whom you've been sold, will be arriving to collect you in two days' time."

Abby gasped, as did Kitty, "She, she sold me? I—I am not a slave! My own momma wasn't even a slave. She was freed, right Kitty?"

"How could she do this? Who is this Mr. Bloomberg?" Kitty bravely demanded, as she slid across the wagon seat, making room for Mr. Allen, who would be riding with them to the train depot. She wrapped a comforting arm around her sister who sat shaking.

"Mr. Bloomberg is one of the richest, most notorious con-artists, and owner of saloons from here all the way to Colorado." He said as he handed the rectangle box to Abby and climbed into the wagon, taking the reins from Kitty.

"You mean to say..." began Kitty.

"...that she sold me to be a whore?" finished Abby, lowering her head in defeat.

"There is no other explanation, which is why we must get you to the train depot and as far away from here as possible," explained Mr. Allen as he set the wagon in motion once again. "I promised your father upon his death bed that I would see to the safety of his girls, and I will not break that promise."

Within moments they had arrived at the train depot, where Mr. Allen helped them both from the wagon. "The train leaves in twenty minutes. You'll need to quickly say your goodbyes and get Abby tucked safely onto that train."

"Thank you, Mr. Allen, for all you've done," said Abby, as he again handed her the white rectangle box. Kitty took it and she and Abby walked toward the train hand in hand. The train was massive and smoke billowed from its smokestack. They stared in awe, having never traveled by train before. They watched as the other travelers milled about, laughing and crying, as they parted ways.

"Kitty?"

"Yes, Abby?" The words stuck in her throat. How could she send her Abby away?

"Don't you see now? I'm different. Please come with me. What if this, this Samuel you wrote to won't accept me after all? What then, Kitty? What do I do?" Abby whimpered.

"Abby, come here." Kitty reached out her arms and wrapped her sister in them, hugging her tightly, wishing she never had to let her go.

"I'd be all alone Kitty, I—I don't think I can do this." Abby sobbed into her shoulder.

"Sadly, Abby, you don't have a choice, and neither do I. Samuel will accept you. You must have faith. I will only be a few short days behind you, and then we'll be together again. I vowed to your mother that I would protect you with my life, and I aim to do just that Abby. I need you to be brave for a short time while I settle the affairs here." Kitty reached down and picked up Abby's carpetbag and placed it over her good arm—the arm Natalie hadn't broken, then handed her the white rectangular box. She hugged her once more as they approached the steps to the train car. The pain in her chest seared as she let go.

"Be so very brave, Abby. You can do this. I know you can. I will be there soon; a Mr. Black will be expecting his bride." Kitty put on her best smile for Abby.

Abby nodded once and straightened her shoulders—a trait they'd both inherited from Papa. Abby held her head high and stepped onto the train. The train that would take her away.

Mr. Allen approached and placed his hand on her shoulder. "Abby is far safer on that train than she is here, Kitty. You are doing the right thing."

"I know I am. It just doesn't feel right. I've never been apart from her, not from the moment she was born."

It seemed like yesterday when her father had ushered her into Lucy's room to meet her new sister. Lucy looked exhausted as she weakly lifted her hand and beckoned Kitty to her.

"Kitty," she had said, her voice barely more than a whisper. "I need you to take care of your sister for me."

"Okay, Miss Lucy. Are you leaving, like Momma did?" She struggled with the tears building in the corner of her eyes.

"Yes, Kitty, the Lord is calling me home. Can you love, care, and protect your sister?"

"Umm-mmm." She nodded. "Wh-what is her name?"

Lucy coughed. "What do you want call her?"

"Abby. Can I call her Abby?"

"That's perfect, Kitty. Abigail means: 'my Father's joy'. Promise me, Kitty, you'll love and protect Abby forever."

"I promise."

It had been a big promise for a four-year-old girl to make, but in that moment, Kitty had grown wise beyond her years. She knew what it was like to be without a momma, and she knew how much her new little sister was gonna want her momma, 'cause *she* wanted her momma every day. So, she promised to be the best big sister ever and would protect Abby with her life.

She could still see Lucy kissing Abby's little cheek, just before her eyes closed and never opened again. Kitty hadn't had time to be mad that God had taken Lucy from her or even to cry, because Abby cried enough for both of them. However, today, as she put Abby on the train, sending her thousands of miles away from her, that anger that had been buried for nineteen years began to seep through the cracks. And Kitty realized for the first time that she was beyond mad, she was furious.

CHAPTER 1

tlanta, Georgia 1899

"WHAT NOW, MR. ALLEN?" Kitty asked as she slowly turned from the train that carried her beloved sister away from her. Like her sister, she squared her shoulders, then inhaled deeply, releasing it slowly as if preparing herself for battle. What else could she call it really? It would be a fight and, in the end, she would lose the only home she'd ever known. The home she had shared with her momma, Miss Lucy, Abby, and her Papa. A home that had once been filled with love. Sure, there had been heartbreak and loss, but love had always remained...until that fateful day Natalie walked through the front door.

"First, we give your Pa a proper burial, and then we get you out of here. Rosendale has already been sold, the funds are in your account. The new owners will take possession the day after the funeral. We will give Mrs. O'Byrne the amount of funds your Pa has left her and let her know she has to vacate the property. However, there has been some new developments regarding the situation with Mrs. O'Byrne. I did not want to discuss them in front of the young Miss O'Byrne and cause her further worry." Mr. Allen said as he turned to help Kitty into the wagon, but she stopped and stared at him.

"What new developments could there possibly be? My papa is gone, we've lost our home, and that woman sold my sister."

"Miss Kitty, perhaps you ought to sit down for this." He pleaded as he brushed a piece of straw from his vest.

"Mr. Allen, I handle things better if I'm able to move about. From time to time, I'm required to stomp my feet in frustration. Papa always said, 'Your Irish is showing Kitty dear, ya might wanna tuck that back in a bit.' It was his teasing way of telling me to control my temper." She chuckled at the memory and swiped at the tear that had escaped and ran down her cheek.

"You're not the fainting type, are ya Miss Kitty?" he asked, looking at her cautiously as if to study her mettle.

"Come now, Mr. Allen, how long have you known me? And, I do believe I just told you, I'm Irish." She grinned, "We're made of tough stock. I can handle it, whatever it is."

"We believe Natalie's marriage to your pa was a ruse, and that she is working with a conman—Mr. Bloomberg to be exact. Which means the funds your pa left for her would go to you, as the marriage was under false pretenses and, therefore, illegal. Natalie might be headed to jail instead."

Squeezing her eyes shut for a moment she asked, "What all has she done and would the authorities truly put her in jail? I guess I never thought about a woman going to jail before." She said crossing her arms in front of her.

"Happens more often than most realize, but yes, if caught, Natalie would go to jail. It is believed that Natalie is actually married to Mr. Bloomberg and has been all this time, making her marriage to your father illegal and void, since her real husband is alive and well," said Mr. Allen.

"How is that even possible?" Kitty shouted.

"Keep your voice down, Miss Kitty, we do not want any word getting back to her." He spoke soft but sternly as he reached for Kitty's hand. "Let's get into the wagon, less people to overhear us as we travel down the road." He said, guiding her back toward the wagon.

Kitty climbed into the wagon, her mind spinning. If Natalie was already married, how in the world did she get away with marrying her pa, more than that, why did she even marry her pa? What woman in her right mind would want two husbands, one had to be bad enough. Kitty plopped down on the wagon seat and shook her head. This was too much, and it didn't make any sense. Why would someone do these things?

"Mr. Allen…" She turned and looked up at him. He was such a tall man and, if he were younger—much younger—she might have been attracted to him. "I don't understand. How can she be married to more than one man?"

"There are ways. A young woman sent a report claiming that a woman matching Natalie's description married her pa, a Mr. Johnson. Her pa became ill and passed away after a few months. When the funeral ended, a man who was overly familiar with Natalie showed up. He thanked her for his new girl and said, 'See ya at home, wife.' The young woman had escaped from a saloon. She was badly beaten, and her injuries were severe." He slapped the reins and set the wagon in motion, as Kitty digested his words.

"Where did this happen? Is the young woman okay, could she come to Atlanta and identify Natalie?" Kitty asked, hopeful, though unsure exactly what for.

"Colorado, but Miss Johnson did not survive her injuries,"

Mr. Allen said as he turned the horses toward Father Jacobs house.

"Colorado! If it was Natalie, how did she end up all the way down here in Atlanta?" Kitty asked, the flicker of hope had vanished and, in its place, set a heavy amount doubt. She knew Natalie was a bad seed, but how would anyone prove these accusations, and what could truly be done with Natalie?

"We believe there are more cases like this one, though no-one else has come forward. We've speculated that Natalie travels from state to state, collecting temporary new husbands, wealthy husbands, with young daughters," he said, dryly.

"Temporary husbands?" Kitty could not control the shake in her voice as she spoke. A temporary husband, what exactly did that mean?

"Yes, temporary. They die within a short time. We think Natalie is poisoning them; your pa lived the longest. The deaths appear to be by natural causes or accidents. Natalie then sells the man's daughter or daughters and walks away with everything."

"How many husbands are we about talking here, and where did you get this information, Mr. Allen?" Kitty asked, suddenly curious as to whether or not the story was actually worth a grain of salt. She hadn't heard of anything like it before. Sure, Natalie was hateful and most unpleasant, but murderous? And her papa had been fighting a sickness off and on before he married Natalie.

"Miss Kitty, your pa was a smart man and, while Natalie may have pulled the wool over his eyes for a brief time, she struggled to keep up the farce as time wore on. However, as far as she knows, she succeeded. What she doesn't know is your pa hired a Pinkerton agent, Detective Gibson, several months ago. He's inside." He nodded toward the small house up ahead.

"Do you think she poisoned my papa?" Kitty asked. If Papa hired a Pinkerton agent… A sickening feeling began swirling inside, settling deep into her gut.

"I do," said he answered. "But I have no proof."

"She, she didn't just sell Abby, did she?" Kitty asked, already knowing the answer before Mr. Allen spoke it.

"No, Miss Kitty, she didn't." He said and looked away as if refusing to look her in the eye.

"Then why didn't I get on that train with Abby? She begged me to!" Kitty shouted. "You could have buried Papa without me. Wouldn't that have been the safest course of action?" she asked.

"Perhaps, but I believe you are strong enough to help us lay a trap. We hope to capture not only Natalie, but her real husband. After all, you did tell me that you are made of tough stock." He grinned gently. "And your pa believed you were capable of this task."

"He did?" she asked softly as she studied Mr. Allen's face. He may have been closer to her papa's age, but she'd known him since she was in short skirts. He wouldn't lie to her, would he?

"Yes, he did. He believed in you Miss Kitty. He led me to believe that you are rather intuitive, and he may have said you've been busting imaginary crime for years. Now is your chance to do something real, to help real women, and to quite possibly save another young lady from not only losing herself to a life she didn't choose, but also from losing her pa," said Mr. Allen.

"Thank you for telling me, but who is us?" she asked as he pulled the wagon to a stop in front of Father Jacobs's house. Father Jacobs lived behind the Sacred Heart Church in a tiny white house with green shutters and a tidy walkway. It looked out of place next to such a large church, but it fit him perfectly.

Father Jacobs was a short, spry old man, with more energy than those half his age. He had twinkly blue eyes that sparkled behind round wire rimmed glasses, and a neatly trimmed white beard. He was balding, but a few wisps of white hair remained and stood on end when the wind caught them. He always made her smile.

"The *us* is myself, Detective Gibson, Father Jacobs, and Sheriff Riley. Of course, Bart Jones is in on it as well," he said, setting the brake and then stepping down. "I'm sorry I couldn't inform you of this any earlier. There are also a few bounty hunters seeking the man we believe to be her true husband, as well as a known accomplice by the name of Crowley. We do not know if it is a first or last name yet."

She watched as he walked around to her side of the wagon and offered her a hand down. She understood why he hadn't told her of these developments until now; it wasn't that he was keeping secrets from her or afraid she wouldn't be strong enough to pull off whatever the plan was. Kitty had been scheming and planning since the day she learned to walk, she'd often dreamed of being a detective herself. She knew how plans worked. She knew Mr. Allen was protecting her, as she had done Abby. The less that knew the inside details, the better. All she had known until this moment was that Rosendale would be sold and she would be in Oregon with Abby, both married to men they didn't know.

"I understand, Mr. Allen," she said and once again squared her shoulders.

Mr. Allen smiled. "I thought you might. Shall we go in? We do not have much time left to discuss things and we do not want Natalie becoming suspicious of your whereabouts." He said, offering her his arm.

Kitty nodded as she took his extended arm. They walked

up to Father Jacobs's door just as the man himself opened it and joyfully welcomed them inside. It seemed to her that Father Jacobs excitable nature had intensified. If she wasn't already aware of Father Jacobs exuberant nature, she would have been taken back.

"Forgive me, Miss O'Byrne. I've never had a secret mission take place in my home before. I know we have sad things to discuss as well. Do come in." He stood to the side, holding the door open. "Hello, Mr. Allen. Nice to see you again."

As Kitty stepped into the small sitting room, a tall, lean man with short dark brown hair and a matching set of deep eyes stood up. He seemed nearly too tall for Father Jacobs's tiny home. His face was clean shaven, his lips were formed into a thin line. Profound creases formed across the bridge of his long nose, probably from the stress of his job. He certainly looked like a detective, she thought.

He reached out his hand. "Miss O'Byrne, I presume."

"Yes," Kitty responded as she shook his hand.

"I'm Detective Gibson, your father hired me. I'm sorry for your loss."

"Thank you. Mr. Allen explained to me that my papa had hired you. What I would like to know, however, is how do you intend to keep me safe? I have to get to Oregon as quickly as possible, my sister is expecting me. She will be greatly worried if I don't arrive next week." She stated, leaving off the fact that a groom was also expecting her. She had yet to come to terms with her impending marriage, so why speak of it?

"We believe that Natalie's real husband, Mr. Bloomberg, or an employee of his, will be arriving the day after the funeral, according to a correspondence Natalie received," said Detective Gibson.

"You read her mail?"

"We intercepted a telegram for Natalie, before it was delivered to her. I would like you to know that you will be able to bury your father in peace tomorrow. However, when Abby does not appear, Natalie could become more troublesome for you. After all, the man is coming to collect two young women. We do not believe she will harm you, as you are now her only meal ticket, so to speak," Detective Gibson stated.

"Meal ticket or not, it won't matter." Kitty knew there was a slight edge to her voice as she spoke, but if Detective Gibson really thought that woman would not harm her, he was dead wrong. Natalie would beat her just for spite. "Natalie broke Abby's arm when I snuck her up to see our papa shortly before he passed. So forgive me if I don't believe you, Detective Gibson," she said as she took her seat.

"I'm sorry miss, I was unaware of that information." He looked toward Mr. Allen before returning to his own seat. "Our reports do not mention any violence from Natalie."

"It was not common knowledge. Only Ms. Lena, our cook, knew about it. She's the one that treated Abby as Natalie would not allow me to send for a doctor. When papa could no longer get up from his sick bed, Natalie banished Abby to the servant quarters. She treated Abby as a slave instead of a daughter. Therefore, I do not believe the physical well being of a young woman matters much to Natalie or to whomever she is selling the women to, if she is indeed doing as you say."

"Miss O'Byrne, do you not believe her capable of these crimes?" Detective Gibson asked, his tone serious.

"Oh, I know exactly what she is capable of, Detective. The woman is pure evil," Kitty responded coldly.

Father Jacobs sat down next to her, taking her hand into his wrinkly one. "Kitty, we are all very sorry about your pa, he was a great man. We know you are hurting something awful, but we are all here to help you and to uncover the truth. You do want that, don't you? To know the truth and prevent other young ladies from going through a similar fate?" he asked gently, his twinkly blue eyes full of compassion.

"Yes, I do, Father. I just, I've lost my papa, my sister, and my home. Please forgive me if I sound a little ungrateful. That is not the case at all. I simply do not think everyone is aware of Natalie's true nature. That is one thing I can bring to this investigation. I have lived with her for nearly a year." She squeezed his hand, then let go and stood.

Pacing within Father Jacob's small home was tricky, but she found it was easier to process things when at least standing. "Gentlemen, with this new information and the inside knowledge I have of Natalie, and though it is barbaric, could she be attempting to break the young women down before someone comes to collect them?" Kitty asked. "It may be that the young ladies would be less likely to fight back."

She assumed none of them had thought of such a thing and, in some twisted way, she wondered if Natalie's cruelty hadn't been an act of kindness. Perhaps, Natalie herself had been a saloon girl and being mean was preparing them for the life they were unknowingly about to live. But, if that were true, why would Natalie sell all those girls to begin with?

"So, what is the plan?" Kitty asked, breaking the deep silence that had enveloped the room as they each became lost in their own thoughts. She had things to do and no time to sit there in silence, wondering about what if's and what nots. It wouldn't get any of them anywhere, that was for sure.

Sheriff Riley cleared his throat, startling Kitty who looked at him. How had she not seen him sitting there? Oh yes, the ever-imposing Detective Gibson had distracted her.

"Miss O'Byrne, first I'd like you to know we've deputized Bart Jones. He works for you correct?"

"Yes Sheriff, he does. He said he would keep Abby and I safe, but I had no idea he'd been deputized."

"He has been feeding us bits of information. Deputizing him is mainly a form of precaution."

Mr. Allen spoke up. "In the event that Mr. Jones should need to apprehend Natalie or whoever shows up, we'd like him to have that authority."

"I see. Is Mr. Jones my only deputized employee?" Kitty asked, wondering how Bart would keep her safe and arrest two others at the same time.

Again, Mr. Allen spoke. "He is the only one your pa trusted, and the only one with this information."

She turned toward Sheriff Riley. "Sheriff, how is one man supposed to protect me and apprehend two others? That does not seem plausible. Furthermore," Kitty took a moment to look each of the men in the eye, "while I appreciate every-thing you are all doing, I would like to know the real driving force behind this. Many would be willing to turn a blind eye to young women disappearing. Apparently many already have, otherwise how would Natalie and this Mr. Bloomberg have gotten away with it all?"

"If I may, Sheriff Riley," Detective Gibson said. "I think I can answer Miss O'Byrne's questions."

"Be my guest," Sheriff Riley said as Kitty watched him relax into his seat. It was interesting how a few questions could make the Sheriff sweat in his boots—some Sheriff he was. The ever-confident Detective Gibson, however, seemed unshaken. She wondered what it would take to rattle such a fearless man, not that she cared to try.

"Miss O'Byrne, you are correct that many would look the other way, but these women have families and friends who have reported them missing. They did not choose the lifestyle they've been thrown into. Several reports indicate their fathers had remarried, yet the new wife has vanished into thin air each time. The only thing that remains the same is the description of one female and her name, Natalie. I requested this case as I thought it might lead me to the whereabouts of my niece, Shannon. I am personally invested in this case, I care about these young women. They need someone willing to step up on their behalf, are you able to assist me in that?" Detective Gibson asked.

"I'm sorry to hear about your niece. I—I didn't know. I do know if someone had taken my sister, I would stop at nothing to find her. Therefore, it would be my honor to assist you and I think it would make my papa proud." She smiled softly. "Though, I do need to get to Oregon as quickly as possible. I have a promise to keep and I don't break my promises, Sir."

"Nor do I, Miss O'Byrne. All we need is for you to remain here until the day after the funeral. We'll be watching the train depot for arrivals, and we have been stationed between here and Rosendale. We want to catch this guy when he shows up to collect you, and that, in itself, will partly convict Natalie of her crimes. We'll take your statement and you can be on your way," said Detective Gibson.

"So, I won't actually be alone. You'll have eyes on me the whole time?" Kitty asked, a bit of relief settling into her chest, making it easier for her to breathe.

"Yes, ma'am," Detective Gibson and Sheriff Riley said in unison.

CHAPTER 2

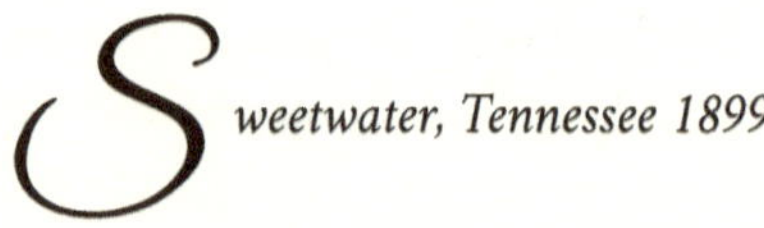

S *weetwater, Tennessee 1899*

"Mr. De Luca! Mr. De Luca!" called out a young boy as he ran down the dusty boardwalk toward him. Milo stopped and waited for him to catch up.

"A telegram for you, sir. Mr. Turpin said you wanted it right away," The lad said as he hunched over to catch his breath, holding up the telegram.

Milo stifled a chuckle as he reached out and took it.

"Sorry, sir, that one plum winded me. Ol' Frank said you were at the inn getting some grub, but Miss Dolly said you'd done skedaddled on out to give your horse some treats, and then Mr. Wilson said you'd done skedaddled on outta there too and headed for the bath house. I sure is glad I found ya, I was getting mighty tired a running, and I didn't wanna interrupt your bath."

"Well, thank you, young man. I sure appreciate it," Milo

said and tipped him generously, after all, the poor boy had just run all over town looking for him. For a brief moment, he wondered what it would be like to have an energetic son. He quickly shook the thought away; he had no time for such foolish thoughts. Having a son meant settling down with a wife and taking the risk of not being able to protect either one of them. It was a risk he wasn't willing to take.

"Thank you, sir."

Milo smiled and watched as the messenger turned to walk back in the direction he'd just come. He unfolded the telegram.

NATALIE ARRESTED. CROWLEY DEAD.
BLOOMBERG SPOTTED, WESTBOUND TRAIN FOR
OREGON.
- GIBSON

What the devil! Milo had been tracking Crowley and Bloomberg to Georgia, and now he had to turn around and go the opposite direction. Sometimes he hated the life of a bounty hunter. But at least tracking down bad guys was easier than being responsible for a whole town full of women and children, as say, a sheriff or a marshal. Though he might enjoy the slower pace of life, he didn't want to be responsible for anyone, other than himself, ever again. Gibson understood that and their mutual investment in Bloomberg didn't hurt matters any.

Bloomberg was more squirrely than a junebug and seemed to have more lives than a cat. He was always two steps head and never in one place long. The question, however, was why Bloomberg was headed to Oregon? His reach didn't go past the state of Colorado, though that hadn't helped any in catching the crook. Every time they had him in their crosshairs, Bloomberg would vanish and pop up three states over. All Milo could do was pray that, eventually, Bloomberg would slip up and make a mistake. Just one mistake was all they needed. Perhaps they were about to get it, now that Bloomberg's right-hand man, Crowley, was gone.

Milo sighed and turned away from the bath house. The bath would have to wait, he needed to send a telegram to his contact in Colorado. Hopefully, Gus would have some information that could, at least, point him to the right part of Oregon. Once he sent the telegram he'd go back and get that overdue bath. He was tired of being on the receiving end of the foul looks from the ladies or the reprimands of the old biddies. They sure had sharp eyes and tongues. He couldn't help that sometimes he smelled like he'd been on a cattle drive. Bad guys moved fast and if he wanted a payday, he had to be quicker.

Soon as he got a hot bath, he was gonna have a nice meal and a good night's sleep. If all went according to plan, he'd have a response by morning and be on the next west-bound train, rested and refreshed. What more could he ask for?

His spurs jangled against the boardwalk as he made his way to the telegraph office. Sweetwater was one of the friendlier little towns he'd visited recently. He enjoyed their slower pace of life, their pleasant atmosphere, and welcoming nature. If he were the settling down type, a place like this wouldn't be a bad idea. Up ahead he watched as two young boys ran full speed to the general store, the younger one bumping an older man as he ran by.

"Sorry, Granpa Joe!" the little tike hollered as he darted into the store, the bell ringing as he ran through.

"Young whippersnappers. Always running everywhere, never lookin' where they go," Milo heard the old man say.

"Hey stranger," the other man called out to Milo, "Did young Ben find ya? That telegraph you's waitin' on came in."

"That he did. How's the checker game going?" Milo asked with a grin. What was it about old timers sitting out front of general stores playing checkers? There seemed to be a pair of them in each of the small towns Milo had passed through over the years. They were often the best eyes and ears in a town. Though one was generally grumpier while the other was the more talkative type.

"Ol' Frank here thinks he's got me beat, but little Bobby just messed a couple of his pieces up and in my favor," the man who Milo assumed was Granpa Joe answered.

"I can still beat ya, old timer." Smirked Frank as the two boys came rushing back out of the store, each with a piece of red licorice in hand, and grinning ear to ear.

"Look Granpa Joe!" The smallest boy held up his candy. "Ben gave us money for a piece of candy." He beamed as he bit off a piece.

"Well, I hope you thanked him for sharing his hard-earned money with you young'uns." Granpa Joe gave them a stern but gentle look.

He must be the grumpy one, thought Milo, but it looked like he had a soft heart he was trying to hide.

"Oh, we did, Granpa Joe," the older one piped. "And I made sure Bobby told Miss Aimee thank you, too. And we didn't mess up her store, neither," he said proudly as he puffed out his little chest.

"That's mighty fine of ya, Billy. I'm glad to see you boys minding your manners," Granpa Joe said as he reached over and ruffled Billy's straw-colored hair.

Ol' Frank tucked his smoke pipe into the front pocket of his overalls and glanced up at Milo. "Bobby and Billy here, are Ben's little brothers. I got me an inklin' that you are the one that made these little fellas' day."

"Hey Mister, why you wearin' that dirty ol'e coat?" Bobby asked as he bit off another piece of the licorice.

Milo knelt down to Bobby's level and looked him in the eye. "Well, young man, I do a lot of traveling and this here coat, it protects my guns from all that dirt."

"My momma would skin me alive if my coat were that dirty." Bobby shuttered.

Milo laughed and noticed Billy had inched closer to him.

"Are you a marshal?" Billy asked. "I'm gonna be a marshal someday. I can shoot real good, my pa even said so," Billy announced pulling his shoulders back as he stood a little taller.

"No, I'm not a marshal, but I bet you'd make a fine one someday." Milo winked at him.

"Are you a bad guy, then?" Little Bobby asked, stepping forward to inspect Milo. "You kinda look like a bad guy. You're all dirty and you wear a black hat instead of a white one. Billy says the good guys wear white hats." Bobby stepped closer and eyed Milo, then reached up with his sticky little hand and patted Milo's cheek. "You need a shave, but you don't got no mean eyes like a bad guy."

"Nosy little fellas, aren't they?" Ol' Frank laughed and Granpa Joe joined him. Milo had a feeling the two old timers were enjoying this far more than their game of checkers. It was a little unnerving to have them all watching him so closely, like a bug caught in a glass jar, as he sat there under the observation of the smallest boy. He wondered, for a moment, if this youngster could actually see into his soul. Perhaps souls appeared to children in black and white colors like hats. Milo knew all about men with mean eyes, but what did little Bobby know about fellas like that?

"Nah, Bobby. I ain't a bad guy. I hunt the bad guys. You sound like you're a pretty good investigator," Milo said, hoping he explained things in a way the little tike might understand. He didn't have much experience with kids, though he liked 'em just fine.

Bobby scrunched up his face. "What's an in-bes-a-gator?"

"A person who asks a whole lot of questions, like you do," Ol' Frank told Bobby.

Billy piped up then. "Like a bounty hunter? I've heard the sheriff talk about 'em."

"That's right, Billy, very impressive," Milo said.

"Is there a bad guy in Sweetwater? Is that why you're here?" Billy asked, the concern for his home written across his little face. He was smart and observant. He certainly would make a fine marshal someday.

"No, son, the bad guy isn't here, and I wouldn't let him hurt y'all if he was." Milo moved his coat slightly, showing one of his guns to Billy, hoping he would feel reassured.

"Was he here?" Bobby asked and continued in rapid fire, "That why you didn't take a bath? You gotta go chase him? Want me and Billy to help ya? We're good chasers, ask Granpa Joe."

"Nah, fellas, he wasn't here, but he ain't where I thought he was, either. I might have to chase him all the way to Oregon, and that's a mighty long way from here. I gotta send another telegram to make sure, and it's gonna be real important I get the response, quick as lightning. Think you boys can help your brother Ben get it to me when it comes in? It'd sure help me out."

"Yup, we can help, can't we, Billy? We're good helpers, right Granpa Joe?" Bobby asked.

"That's right, Bobby. You boys better skedaddle on and tell Ben now." Granpa Joe ushered them off.

"Alright, Granpa Joe. Let's go, Billy." Little Bobby said, tugging at his arm.

"I hope you catch the bad guy, mister," Billy said. He was the quieter one of the two, another reason he'd make a good marshal. He listened, and viewed everything cautiously.

"Me too, Billy, and you can call me Milo." He tipped his hat and Billy nodded, then trotted off with his brother.

Granpa Joe glanced up from his checkers. "Your good with them, got a son back home?"

"No sir, life of a bounty hunter doesn't leave much room for settling down and raising a family. I best get this telegram sent. A word of advice though, you can beat Ol' Frank there in two moves."

Milo grinned and walked on down to the telegraph office, wondering if it was time to hang his hat. He was tired, tired of chasing fellas all over the country, and tired of sleeping with one eye open. The idea of settling down with a pretty little wife to snuggle up to on cold nights, and a passel full of children to watch over and teach, seemed to be plaguing him. He needed to stuff that idea back down where it belonged and concentrate on the job at hand. A wife and children were a pleasant dream, nothing more.

He shook the thoughts from his head as he opened the door to the telegraph office. The bell above the door rang and Mr. Turpin looked up from the desk.

"Ah, Mr. De Luca, back already?"

"Yes, I need to send another telegram, this one to Colorado."

"Right-o, what would you like it to say?" Mr. Turpin pulled a pencil from behind his ear and held it above a pad of paper.

D.B. OREGON BOUND.
CONFIRM LOCATION.
- DE LUCA

"That oughta do it, Mr. Turpin. If you could send young

Ben with the response when it comes in, I'd sure appreciate it." Gus would know who and understand what he was asking, so Milo didn't feel the need to expand further.

"Sure thing, Mr. De Luca. You gonna be any place particular?"

"Thank you. I'm headed back to the bath house and then I'll be at the inn." Milo laid a coin down on the counter and headed back out the door.

* * *

MILO WALKED into the dining room of the inn, feeling far more respectable than he had earlier in the day, when he'd been covered in travel grime. He chose a table near the window and sat facing the entrance. It wouldn't do to be caught unaware, though he felt rather relaxed here. He'd not seen one ounce of trouble. He watched as Mrs. Dolly delivered a bowl of soup to a corner table, then turned and headed his direction.

"Well now, I almost didn't recognize ya, sonny." Mrs. Dolly smiled as she wiped her hands on her apron. "Would you like the special tonight? We got chicken fried steak with mashed taters and gravy, fresh green beans, and slice of cherry pie for dessert. Or you can have the soup?"

"Tempting as that..."

Mrs. Dolly started laughing and pointed at the window, where two matching pairs of sapphire eyes peeked in.

"Ben! We found him, he shaved, but it's him." They pointed at Milo and then ran for the entrance.

Milo shook his head. "Mrs. Dolly, do them little fellas ever slow down?"

Mrs. Dolly started laughing harder and held her stomach. "No sir, them ones are only still when they're sleeping. They're poor momma, they wear her plum out." She pointed toward the entrance where all three boys stood waiting politely, albeit impatiently. They practically danced as they waited for Milo to meet them.

Milo followed her finger to the boys and back again. "Why'd they stop?"

"They know better than to run through my dining room, Mr. De Luca. Now, before I let them come over here, why don't you tell me what you want for dinner? Cook can get it going while you conduct your business." She winked.

"I'll have the special, ma'am."

"Smart man. Coffee, tea, or water?"

"Coffee."

"I'll be back in a jiffy." Then she walked toward the three boys. Milo didn't know what she said to them, but they slowly walked—in a single file line—straight to his table.

"Evening fella's, would you like a seat?" Milo asked and the two young ones sent pleading looks to their brother Ben as they waited for him to answer. It was then that Milo realized Ben had the same startling blue eyes. Normally, he wouldn't have noticed such a thing. Someday these little fellas would have the ladies falling at their feet.

"For a moment, then we gotta get home. Momma is gonna have dinner ready," Ben told them and waited for them to sit down before he joined them. "I got your telegram. It came in right before Mr. Turpin closed up for the day." He reached in his pocket and handed the wrinkled-up note to Milo.

"Thank you, Ben, I appreciate you bringing it here to me," Milo said, taking the note and tucking it into his shirt pocket.

"Least I didn't have to chase ya all over town this time."

"And we helped ya find him didn't we, Ben?" said Bobby, turning to Milo. "Say, where's your dirty coat?"

"Bobby," Ben fussed.

"What? He said it protects his guns and he ain't wearing it no more."

"Well Bobby, Mrs. Dolly runs a pretty clean establishment here. I don't think my guns will get dirty in here and my coat did need a washing. Plus, I wouldn't want to mess it up for her. Don't think she'd take too kindly to that, do you?"

"No sir, she wouldn't," all three boys responded.

"It sure did need washed. You wouldn't want my ma to have seen it." Bobby shuddered again like he had earlier in the day, and Milo smiled.

"Did you get your coat all dirty, Bobby?" Milo asked and a blush crept across Bobby's little face as he hung his head.

"He did more than get it dirty. He rolled around in a mud hole after a big rain." Billy confirmed. "He keeps it real clean now."

"I bet so. Momma's don't like messes do they boys?"

"No sir!" They all three said in unison.

"We'd best get home. Ma won't be happy if we're late." Ben said as he stood up.

Milo reached in his pocket and tipped Ben, then gave a penny to Billy and Bobby. "That's for helping Ben find me. You fella's stay outta trouble now, and keep those coats clean."

"Yes sir. Thank you, sir." They all said and then left the dining room as slowly as they'd entered it. Milo smiled, and soon as the door of the inn closed, the boys took off in a dead run. He shook his head and had to laugh at the thought: *Ma's don't understand dirty coats.*

"Told ya them boys never slow down," Mrs. Dolly said as she set his plate on the table.

"How'd you get them to stop and walk in here so calmly?" Milo asked.

"They like to visit me during the day for a treat. They won't get one if they run in my dining room." She winked.

"Enjoy your meal, Mr. De Luca," she said and headed back toward the kitchen.

Milo cut into his chicken fried steak and took a bite, savoring the flavors and warmth it provided. He was curious as to what Gus had to say, but he didn't like to eat cold food, either. He cut another piece and dipped it into the creamy gravy covered mashed potatoes before taking a bite. The food was good, really good, and Milo knew he'd sleep well tonight for sure.

As he ate his meal, he enjoyed the homey atmosphere. Everyone knew the other and had welcomed him immediately. He imagined it was similar to having a large family dinner. Mrs. Dolly, who flit from table to table, refilling drinks and taking orders, would be the family matriarch. The one who took care of them all, making sure their bellies were full and their coffee hot. He took a drink of his now and thought back to the note in his pocket. He set his cup down and pulled it out. He didn't look forward to heading out of such a friendly town so soon. He'd rather eat Mrs. Dolly's fine cooking than hardtack and cold sandwiches, but he did have a job to do. At least he'd get one good night's sleep before he set out again. He sighed and unfolded the note.

D.B. AFTER AKECHETA JAMES.
SILVERPINES OREGON.
GUS

So that's why Bloomberg was headed to Oregon. Now, it made sense; Bloomberg had a sister, Nancy. She had been engaged to Pastor Akecheta James. Sadly, the morning before the wedding, Nancy took her own life. She'd been ill for some time, though few knew about it. Bloomberg blamed Akecheta simply because of his heritage, though he was innocent of any wrong doing and everyone knew it. Milo tucked the note back in his pocket, took one last drink of coffee, left a tip on the table for Mrs. Dolly, and headed up to bed. There was nothing more he could do tonight, and he needed rest before beginning his journey northwest. Perhaps, he'd catch a few other wanted men as he made his way across the country. And maybe he'd shake the longing the town of Sweetwater had stirred up in him.

CHAPTER 3

hree days earlier.

KITTY STOOD before the gravesite and listened as Father Jacobs spoke. "Peace I leave with you, my peace I give unto you: not as the world giveth, give I unto you. Let not your heart be troubled, neither let it be afraid..." She wanted to rest in the words Father Jacobs shared, but her heart was broken and terribly troubled. Not only that, she was quite frightened, though she put on a tough face.

She couldn't believe the things she'd learned about Natalie, or that her papa had possibly been poisoned. It was true her papa had been sick and was declining, but if Natalie had poisoned him, it would have increased the speed of his sickness, taking him away from her and Abby before either were ready. Would she have ever been ready, though? She missed him. She missed Abby, too. Abby should have been with her today.

Kitty watched as the first shovel of dirt fell upon her

papa's coffin and couldn't remember a time she'd ever felt so alone. He had been her one true constant but now he was gone forever. She would no longer hear the tilt of Irish upon his tongue or feel the safety in his warm hugs. Papa had been the foundation on which her little family stood. How did one remain standing with the foundation missing? What was she supposed to do now?

She knew what she was *supposed* to do; help lay the trap to catch Natalie and whoever arrived, and then hightail it to Oregon. Where she would marry some man she had no desire to marry, just to be near Abby. Why had she agreed to answer the advertisement when Papa had urged her to do so? She didn't want to get married and why should she? Papa left her and Abby plenty of money to survive on.

What if she didn't get married? Maybe if she was late in arriving, the man would change his mind. She could refund his money. As the thought took hold, Kitty found herself liking the idea more and more, but what would she do in Oregon? She had nowhere else to go really. Abby would be married and wouldn't need her like before. Yet, Abby was all she had left, and she'd made a vow, a promise to Miss Lucy, and for those reasons she needed to be near Abby.

The burial service had ended and yet Kitty still remained, standing frozen in the same spot. She had effectively drowned out Natalie's ridiculous wailing. The woman was sure putting on a good show. If only everyone knew what a fraud she was. Kitty felt a hand on her shoulder and turned to see Father Jacobs standing next to her.

"It's time to go, dear. Your pa is with the Lord now, you can take comfort in that," he said.

"I know, Father Jacobs, I just miss him, and I have a whole lot on my mind," Kitty explained, turning from the grave that now held her papa. How would she ever get over losing him? Everyone she had ever loved, minus Abby, had left her. They always leave, she thought. No, she wouldn't be giving her heart to anyone else, not even Mr. Black, though she'd agreed to marry him. It simply hurt too much.

"How 'bout we get us some fresh lemonade and talk a bit? I'm a pretty good listener and I'd like a moment to pray for you before you begin your new adventure." Father Jacobs smiled that big toothy smile and, though she had wanted to be alone, she couldn't turn him down. It might be the last time she saw him.

"Thank you, I'd like that, Father Jacobs," Kitty said and followed him into the large church for a bit of refreshment. The community had come together to mourn the loss of her papa. Kitty was thankful they'd come to show their respects; her papa had been loved.

She didn't have to worry about Natalie yet as she was too busy playing the grieving widow and soaking up all the attention it provided. Kitty had to give it to her, she was a pretty good actress.

For a brief moment, Kitty wondered what would happen to Natalie. Surely, she wouldn't be able to act her way out of all the allegations against her. Yet, what would they do with Natalie once her involvement was proven? She'd never heard of a woman going to jail before.

"Father Jacobs, do you know what will happen to her," she nodded toward Natalie, "tomorrow?"

"No, Miss O'Byrne. I'm not certain. Though, I shall spend my day praying for your safety and her soul," he said as he took a sip of the tart lemonade and made a face. "That first drink gets me every time." He smacked his lips together.

Kitty grinned at him, taking a sip of her own, her eyes watering slightly. He was such a sweet old man. She would miss him. "Father Jacobs, would you like me to write to you once I'm settled?"

"Why, I would love that. After all, I've known ya since you

were a wee babe. I'd like to know that you are safe and happy and how Miss Abby is fairing."

"Then, I shall."

* * *

KITTY SAT ALONE at the dining room table, pushing the breakfast Ms. Lena had served her around the plate with her fork. She thought the enormity of her grief would have come crashing in on her like the waves from the Georgia hurricane that destroyed the lives of more than 170 people last year, ripping some of them away into watery graves. Lost forever. Yet only single tears fell, one by one. She brushed them away, perhaps a little too harshly, frustrated by their appearance. She didn't want them there, falling from her eyes and sticking to her cheeks, glistening like beacons announcing her pain for all the world to see. Not that anyone was there.

Kitty had stopped crying the day Miss Lucy died. She'd had to take care of Abby, to protect her, that meant she had to be strong. She had no time for tears, what was the point in them anyway, and why were these rogue ones falling now? There was no one to comfort her, even if she were to let them fall without abandon. Her papa wasn't there to soothe her fears anymore. It was just her, alone. In an empty house with an evil woman. The silence of her pain and fears echoed in her ears like her fork scraping against the China plate.

"Are you going to eat your breakfast or play with it?" Natalie demanded.

Startled, Kitty looked up, she hadn't heard Natalie enter the room. At least the woman was wearing mourning clothes today.

"Sorry, I was lost in thought, I guess," Kitty said.

"Well, you should have eaten it. It's probably long cold by now." Natalie said as Ms. Lena entered the room and poured her a cup of hot tea. "You can take Kitty's plate, she's finished, and I cannot handle the screeching of that fork!"

"Yes, Ma'am." Ms. Lena said as she approached and retrieved the plate. Kitty didn't care. She knew she should have eaten. Ms. Lena was the best cook in the county, but Kitty's stomach had only rolled and rebelled. Many people had tried to steal Ms. Lena away from them but Papa had enjoyed her food too much to let that happen. The fact that both his girls were equally fond of Ms. Lena perhaps had a bit of sway, too.

Kitty wondered if the new owners would be keeping Ms. Lena or if the older woman had other plans, perhaps she'd move on to Tennessee where some of her family lived. They hadn't discussed it. She'd ask her later that day. Maybe, if she gave Ms. Lena the funds that had been set aside for Natalie, she could retire and enjoy growing old with her family nearby.

She looked up then to see Natalie had not taken her seat, but stood near the window, tea cup in hand as she looked out. Kitty knew she was expecting someone and probably hoping that particular someone did not arrive until after Mr. Allen had read Papa's will.

"When is that incompetent lawyer of your father's supposed to arrive?" Natalie asked.

"He did not give me a time. He only said today," Kitty said. "Did you have plans?"

"Well, no, but I don't want to be kept waiting all day, either," Natalie fussed, as she fiddled with the rim of her teacup.

Kitty was relieved to see that she wasn't the only nervous one, although for an entirely different matter. She knew Mr. Allen would be arriving shortly, before the train was due in town. They would be inside going over the details of her papa's estate. Sheriff Riley and his men would be watching the train depot and spaced out along the way to Rosendale. Detective Gibson was out there somewhere, too, along with the newly deputized Bart Jones. She was entrusting her life into the hands of these few men. Papa had trusted them and that was good enough for her.

"It's about time," Natalie said as she stepped away from the window, set her teacup down, and smoothed out her black mourning dress. Kitty could hear the horse approaching and knew without standing that Mr. Allen had arrived, and within ten minutes she was sure to hear the train whistle. It was most likely an inappropriate thought, but she was looking forward to watching Natalie squirm after all the woman had put her family through.

She heard the knock at the door but remained seated, knowing Ms. Lena would see Mr. Allen in. Natalie sat down at the table and twiddled with her napkin, though she had eaten no breakfast, either.

Ms. Lena stepped into the dining room. "Mr. Allen is here to see you, Ma'am."

Natalie stood as he walked with his briefcase in hand, and still Kitty chose to remain seated. She saw no reason to stand.

"Mrs. O'Byrne, thank you for seeing me today," Mr. Allen said.

"Well, you didn't give me much of a choice, now did you? What I'd like to know is why do we have to discuss these matters today? My poor husband was only laid to rest yesterday," Natalie said, and Kitty watched as the pretend tears began to well up in Natalie's eyes.

"I'm sorry, Ma'am, but there are matters that must be immediately addressed. Shall we sit?" asked Mr. Allen.

"Very well." Natalie groaned.

Mr. Allen laid his briefcase on the table and unlatched it, removing the documents and latching it back before setting it aside. He opened a folder and pulled out a sheaf of documents.

"This is the last will and testament of Mr. Angus Patrick O'Byrne of Atlanta, Georgia, dated April first, eighteen-ninety-nine." Mr. Allen cleared his throat. "As my lovely daughters, Miss Kathleen Elizabeth O'Byrne and Miss Abigail Jane O'Byrne, will both marry this summer, I have sold Rosendale plantation to Mr. Barnaby Danvers."

"Well, I never!" shouted Natalie as she stood. "How could he do that to me, and where am I supposed to live, since when are *you* getting married?"

"Since Papa arranged it," Kitty said.

"Did you know about this?" Natalie demanded.

"Yes, I did. Papa told me he was selling Rosendale."

"And that-that sister of yours, where is she?"

"Already married," Kitty said.

"Why you, you little conniving…"

"I only did as Papa instructed me to do," Kitty said, cutting her off.

"Mrs. O'Byrne if we could please continue…" Mr. Allen said.

Shots rang out in the distance, causing Kitty to jump. She watched as Natalie ran to the window.

"What is going on out there? Who is shooting?" Natalie asked as Bart Jones raced in from the side door, "What are you doing in here?"

Bart ignored her. "Shots fired, east side," Bart told Mr. Allen

"Guard Miss O'Byrne."

"What about me?" Natalie wailed.

"Not to worry, Ma'am, I won't be letting you out of my sight," said Mr. Allen.

Kitty watched as a multitude of emotions flashed across Natalie's face. She couldn't tell if Natalie was relieved or frightened. It didn't matter much as she wouldn't be letting the vile woman out of her sight, either. She may not know exactly how to use the small derringer she held beneath the table, but she refused to go down without a fight.

The pounding of horse hooves drew closer. The truth would be revealed in a moment and she couldn't wait, she had a train to catch. The further she got away from here the better. Kitty was stunned by the sudden thought, but realized it was true. There was nothing left for her here. One might say she was running from the pain, but she was ready for an adventure of her own, and longed to see Abby.

"Deputy Jones," Sheriff Riley called, "we're all good here!"

Detective Gibson entered the dining room. "Everyone alright in here?" he asked.

"Who-who is that man lain across that horse?" Natalie asked, her voice shaking as she pointed out the window.

"Well now, *Mrs. Bloomberg*, that would be your real husband's right-hand man, Crowley," said Detective Gibson.

Natalie crumbled to the ground in dead faint. Crowley's appearance had sealed her fate.

Kitty was thankful that Detective Gibson and Sheriff Riley had kept her safe. She smiled now as she noticed the gun Mr. Allen wore. It looked out of place on him.

She reached out her hand and placed it on Bart's arm. "Thank you, Deputy Jones."

"I told ya, Ma'am, we wouldn't let nothing happen to you or Miss Abby," Bart said.

"Are you staying on here with the new owners or have you decided on a new profession?" Kitty asked.

"Little of both, Ma'am. You have a safe trip to Oregon now, ya hear?"

"Thank you, Bart."

Bart nodded and left. Natalie moaned and Detective

Gibson reached down, taking her by the arm and into custody.

"Thank you, Miss O'Byrne, for your assistance," he said and escorted Natalie out the door.

"Well, Miss O'Byrne, shall we head into town? I believe you have a room booked at the hotel and your train leaves tomorrow morning. Miss Abby will sure be happy to see you," said Mr. Allen.

"Mr. Allen, the funds that were originally going to Natalie, could you give them to our cook, Ms. Lena?" Kitty asked.

"Yes Ma'am, I can arrange that," he said.

"Then give me just a moment, I wish to tell her and to say goodbye," Kitty said and rushed from the dining room into the kitchen. Ms. Lena was sitting at the counter, tears streaming down her chubby face.

"Ms. Lena, are you alright?" she asked.

"Oh yes, dear. I only stayed on for as long as I did because of you girls. You're so precious to me," she said, wiping her tears away with a kitchen towel.

"We will miss you too, Ms. Lena, but we have a gift for you."

"Oh, you sweet girls, you didn't have to get me anything. My time with you was gift enough."

"We didn't know your future plans… Papa set aside some funds for Natalie but since she is guilty of serious crimes, we'd like you to have them. You could go see your family in Tennessee or travel, maybe come see Abby and I sometime?" Kitty suggested.

"My dear girl, you do know your pa paid me generously, don't you?"

"No, Ms. Lena, but what I do know is Abby and I have plenty to live on for the rest of our lives, and we want you to have this. I've asked for Mr. Allen to arrange it," Kitty said.

"It would be nice to go home to Tennessee. My sister has three grandsons I haven't seen in quite some time," she said.

"It's settled then." Kitty wrapped Ms. Lena in a big hug. "You are always welcome in Oregon."

"Thank you, Miss Kitty."

The following morning, Kitty stood, once again, on the train platform with Mr. Allen. Ms. Lena had quickly arranged her affairs and would be boarding the train with her. It was an unexpected surprise and she found she was thankful for it.

"Your pa left you this, but you are not to open it until you arrive in Silverpines. You wouldn't want it to get covered in soot and dust from the train." Mr. Allen handed her a white rectangle box like he'd given to Abby.

"Thank you, Mr. Allen, for all you've done." She looked down at the box. "I'm thankful it has come to an end and that I can put it behind me now. I couldn't have done it without you," she said as Ms. Lena came bustling up.

"I made it. I'm here my dear, are we ready for a grand time?" she asked. "Oh my, look at the people. I'd say it's going to be a bit crowded."

"I'll let you ladies get settled. Miss O'Byrne, should you need anything you have my information," he said.

"Thank you, Mr. Allen," Kitty said, leaning in to hug him goodbye. "I'll miss you," she whispered.

"And I you," he said flatly as Ms. Lena leaned forward, hooking her arm through Kitty's.

"I will take good care of her. Don't you worry." She patted him on the shoulder. "Shall we find our seat dear?" asked Ms. Lena. "It won't be the most comfortable but it's the sacrifice one must make when traveling."

"I reckon we shall." She sniffled, clutching the box to her chest. "Do—do you enjoy train travel Ms. Lena?" Kitty asked as they boarded the long black train, similar to the one Abby left on, and stowed the bags. Looking out the window, she saw Mr. Allen had remained, watching them board with slumped shoulders. She'd lost her pa, had to send her sister far away, lay a trap that frightened her, but never once had she thought about what Mr. Allen had lost until now. Pa and he had been great friends. The heaviness she'd been wishing would disappear settled into her chest, causing her to rub her fist against her heart as she fought for relief. She lost too, but she could have been kinder.

"I do, for short trips," Lena said, digging into her handbag and pulling out a handkerchief. She handed it to Kitty. "It's interesting to watch the different landscapes unfold. You'll see areas just as flat as can be and others that look like they're trying to reach up and touch the heavens. After many days, you do tire of the constant movement and the grime, though." Ms. Lena made a face.

"Oh dear, I hadn't thought about that," said Kitty as the train whistled loudly and lurched forward, causing her to grab hold of the seat before her. Atlanta would be behind her in a moment. It was terrifying, and exciting, and it added to the pain in her chest. She couldn't wait to get to Abby and ensure she was safe, and that her new husband was treating her well. Maybe then she'd feel some sort of relief. In the meantime, she would write an apology to Mr. Allen.

CHAPTER 4

Kitty awoke from a troubled sleep when the conductor called out the next stop. She sat up and smoothed out her hair as she looked to Ms. Lena. "What did he say?" she asked, yawning.

"He said the next stop is Sweetwater, dear. We'll be getting off there."

"Oh! I feel so horrible, I slept most the way."

"You needed your rest dear, you've had a rough few days and I wasn't about to wake you after all you've been through," said Ms. Lena, patting Kitty's arm.

"Thank you. I'm sorry I wasn't much company for you," Kitty said.

"Sweetwater, Tennessee," The conductor called out for a second time. "Those traveling onward have thirty minutes to stretch your legs and enjoy some of Mrs. Dolly's fine cooking," he said, his voice rough, as if he'd gotten smoke in his lungs.

Kitty's stomach rumbled at the mention of food, causing Ms. Lena to chuckle.

"Sounds to me like you might need to grab a bite to eat. I

know you haven't been eating well, but you'll need your energy for this trip. It's gonna be a long one," said Ms. Lena.

"Yes, Ms. Lena, I believe you're right. Do you know a place nearby?" Kitty asked.

"I know the best place. I'd say it is one of the best kept secret around these parts, but that conductor just blabbed it to everyone on this train. My sister, Dolly, owns it. She's an amazing cook. You can help me surprise her." Smiled Ms. Lena

"She couldn't be as good as you. Papa always loved your cooking."

"It's a good thing he didn't find her first. She's better," said Ms. Lena. "The inn is straight across the way there. You won't be far from the train." She gathered her belongings and led the way with a bounce in her step that made Kitty's heart happy. After the past week, she needed that bit of joy to help burn out the pain in her chest.

They walked directly across from the train straight to the inn. It was a quaint little town and so much smaller than Atlanta. Everything was right there on one road. It had a welcoming feel and Kitty found she rather liked it. She wondered why Ms. Lena left it years ago and watched as two young boys ran past.

Ms. Lena turned to her then. "I think that might be my sister's grandsons, Billy and Bobby, but I haven't seen them in ages. They grow so quickly. Dolly is always writing about them and how they run everywhere they go—except her dining room at the inn," said Ms. Lena

They stepped up onto the boardwalk and entered the inn. "Let's just take a seat and see how long it takes her to notice me." Ms. Lena grinned.

Kitty followed along and sat with her back to the door so that Ms. Lena would be able to see the room. She was so intent on watching the surprise unfold that she nearly missed the man dressed in solid black sitting behind Ms. Lena. He was staring directly at her, his dark eyes never wavering as he lifted his coffee cup to meet a pair of full lips.

Kitty looked away, slightly frightened. Who was he? she wondered while picking at the napkin on the table. Unable to stop herself, she glanced back up, her eyes clashing with his beautiful dark chocolate ones. She held his gaze for a moment before looking away again, feeling the heat rush to her cheeks. Oh dear, she'd be bright red in a moment. That was the last thing she wanted him to see.

What if he was Mr. Bloomberg? Did Mr. Bloomberg know what she or Abby looked like? She thought, trying to distract herself from the handsome man. She'd always imagined Mr. Bloomberg to look like a monster, though she truly had no idea, and the man before her was no monster. Something about the man sitting behind Ms. Lena had sent her pulse racing and suddenly she was very thirsty.

"Lena? Is that you?" called out a small plump woman with curly black and gray hair. She wiped her hands on her apron and rushed across the dining room, embracing Ms. Lena in a warm hug.

"Grammie! You said no treats if we run in here," called out a small boy standing at the entrance of the dining room, his little fist balled up on his hips.

"Oh, Bobby, come here. You are correct and I'm sorry. I won't have any dessert with my dinner, but I'd like you to meet my sister, Ms. Lena. She surprised me and that's why I ran. I haven't seen her in a very long time."

"It's okay, Grammie. You can have dessert. I know you's excited and dats why you ran. Dats why I runs everywhere. Is she my grammie, too?" asked Bobby as he looked between the two women.

"Well no..."

"She looks like a grammie. She even has hair like you," Bobby whispered loudly.

Mrs. Dolly smiled and wrapped her arm around Bobby. "Bobby, here, thinks everyone beyond a certain age is his grandparent," she told Ms. Lena.

"That's quite alright. I've never been a grammie. I'd be honored to be one," said Ms. Lena.

Bobby looked at Kitty then. "She's not your grammie?" he asked, his little face showing his confusion. He probably wouldn't appreciate Kitty saying so, but he had the prettiest little blue eyes she had ever seen.

"No, she's not. I never met my grammie."

"Dat's sad, you should keep her for your grammie," said Bobby.

"Ms. Lena has been the cook in my home for many years, so I guess she's kinda like a grammie," said Kitty.

"Oh yes. All grammie's cook." Bobby smiled big, showing a few missing teeth. "Dats what makes them good grammies."

"And she's the best cook, too," said Kitty.

"Are you sure? Cause people's always coming here on that there train to eat *my* grammie's cooking. So, I don't know if I believe you," said Bobby.

"Well Bobby, I'm going to be staying here awhile, how about I make you some treats and you can decide if you like my cooking or not?" said Ms. Lena.

"Can you make a cherry pie?" he asked.

"You want a pie? Not some cookies?"

"Cookies are for babies. I'm a growing man," he stated and pulled on his little suspenders.

Ms. Lena laughed. "A pie it is."

"Alright Bobby, why don't you go on and pick up your lunches from the kitchen, while I see what these hungry travelers would like for lunch," said Mrs. Dolly.

"Okay. Nice to meet you new Grammie. Wait, who are

you?" Bobby asked, looking at Kitty. She glanced up and noticed the stranger still had his dark eyes locked on her. He was clean shaven and had a strong jawline, but those eyes, for a moment she wondered if she should answer Bobby or not, but she didn't want to be rude. It was ridiculous to think the man might be Mr. Bloomberg anyway.

"I'm Kitty. Ms. Lena was keeping me company on the train," she said.

"Oh, are you staying, too?"

"No, I have someplace I've got to be."

"Me too. I'm going fishing with Billy. See ya later," he said and trotted off toward the kitchen.

"That's the inquisitive one, always asking questions," said Mrs. Dolly, reaching out to Kitty. "It sure is nice to finally meet you. Lena has told me all about you and Abby over the years. Is Abby not with you? I'd love to meet her, too."

"She recently married," said Kitty as she glanced up to judge the stranger's reaction, but he only stared and she had a feeling if she gazed too long into those eyes she'd melt.

"Well, I'd best get you some food. How 'bout I bring you both the special; fried chicken, creamy mashed potatoes, a side of green beans, and a slice of apple pie," said Mrs. Dolly.

"Fried Chicken is one of Kitty's favorites," Ms. Lena announced. "Could you put a little something together in a bag for her, as well, she's got a long journey ahead."

"I'd be happy to. See ya in jiffy."

Soon as Mrs. Dolly disappeared, the man that had been staring at Kitty stood. He was the tallest man she'd ever laid eyes on and she had to lean her head back to see just how tall he was. For a tall man, he filled out his frame with thick arms and legs. Like a solid shield of protection versus a string bean that would snap in two. He laid down the money for his bill, tipped his hat to Kitty, and walked out.

Kitty leaned forward. "Ms. Lena, do you know that man?" she asked.

"No dear, I can't say as I've seen him before. Why?"

"He stared at me the whole time. It made me a little nervous," she said, shivering.

"You're a beautiful young lady, Kitty. The fellas are going to notice. But I understand you being a tad uneasy. You just be careful out there and take care of yourself," Ms. Lena said.

"Thank you, I will." She said as Mrs. Dolly approached and set their lunch on the table. It smelled so good that Kitty's stomach rumbled loud enough for both ladies to hear it and Kitty's cheeks grew warm. She was thankful the handsome man had left and not heard her stomach or seen how beet red she'd become.

"You eat up, Miss Kitty, and take this for your journey," said Mrs. Dolly as she handed her a paper bag.

"Thank you, very much," Kitty said.

"Lena, we'll visit after you've said your goodbyes and this lunch crowd has skedaddled on outta here. It was nice to meet you Miss Kitty, you have a safe journey now," she said as she turned and headed back toward the kitchen.

"Better eat up girlie, we've gotta get you back on that train," said Ms. Lena as she dipped her fork into the gravy covered mashed potatoes and sighed. "My sister sure can cook."

Kitty only nodded as she dug into her food and they finished their meal in silence.

Their last few moments together were over far too soon, and it was time for Kitty to board the train, this time alone. She worried that the stranger with the dark eyes would be on the same train. She wouldn't mind seeing him again and that both terrified and excited her. What if he was Mr. Bloomberg? For the second time that day, she wished she had asked Detective Gibson what Mr. Bloomberg looked like.

Ms. Lena walked her back across the road to the train platform, then pulled her into a big hug and held on tight. "If you need anything you let me know, and if you and Abby aren't happy, you come on right back here to Sweetwater and let Ms. Lena take care of y'all," she said.

"Yes Ma'am. I'll send word once I've arrived. Thank you for all you've done," Kitty said as she hugged Ms. Lena one last time before turning to board the train.

CHAPTER 5

*M*ilo watched from the back of the train car as the young woman from the inn boarded. She was tiny, though, to him most people were. He'd be surprised if she even stood five feet tall. Still, who was she and where was she going? He knew he'd been staring at her in the dining room, but he couldn't help it. Her eyes had sparkling flecks of gold in them, and he was having a hard time deciphering their actual color. And her hair. He'd never seen the likes of it. The coppery red strands mixed with dirty brown, and straw-colored hair stood out against her soft porcelain skin as if asking him to run his fingers through it. Never had he been more drawn to a woman than he was in that moment.

She was the loveliest creature he'd ever seen. He knew he'd made her uncomfortable and he should apologize for his rudeness, but he feared she wouldn't accept it. She might quite possibly ignore him all together. His job required him to be fairly good at reading people and the young *bella signorina* seemed to be frightened of something or someone. After setting eyes on her the first time, a wave of fierce protectiveness rose up with an intensity that shocked him out of his stupor, propelling him to the door. He'd left the inn without telling Mrs. Dolly or little Bobby goodbye. He'd have to try to come back through Sweetwater during his travels.

He pulled his black hat down low and sank back into the seat as she neared, taking the seat a few rows ahead of him. He smiled. From here, he could observe her without offending her, and, perhaps, learn more about her and who she was running from. She looked small and fragile as she sat there alone, clutching her paper bag of previsions while watching the other passengers board. He wondered if she were looking for him. The surge of protectiveness rose again —what was it about her? He could tell she wasn't used to traveling. She didn't pull out a book or a knitting project like most women did. No, she was fidgety, as if she were nearing her destination and couldn't wait to get off the train, instead of just beginning her journey. It was probably her first time on a train, alone, since the lady she'd arrived with had stayed behind.

The whistle blew, and the train lurched forward, heading out of Sweetwater and north toward Ohio. Passengers waved at those still standing on the platform and others had already settled in. The crinkle of newspapers unfolding and pages turning filled the air. The soft click of knitting needles were nearly drowned out by the loud clanking of the train. Others chatted and yet, she sat, stiff backed and still clutching her bag.

Milo watched as the young woman fought the sleep that had been trying to claim her for the last hour. Something was bothering her and keeping her awake. She hadn't seen him, and he'd hoped that would ease her mind, but apparently, he was not the demon that kept sleeping beauty awake.

He longed to reach out to her and to offer his assistance, but the last time he'd tried to protect someone he'd failed.

That failure cost him the only family he had left; his baby sister Alessa. He couldn't risk that type of failure again, but he could keep an eye on the little lady.

He watched as her head jerked from the window yet again. If only he hadn't scared her earlier, perhaps she would have felt safe with him. Safe enough to sleep and put an end to her struggle. The train conductor called out the next stop, where most passengers had either reached their final destination or would be changing trains. Milo stood and gathered his meager belongings, making his way forward. The young lady had finally fallen asleep and as he approached he could hear the faint little snores coming from her.

He'd never seen an angel, but if he had, he'd imagine it'd look just like the young woman as she slept. Her coppery golden hair glistening like a halo above her soft porcelain skin, and her sweet strawberry pink lips were open on feathery breaths. He didn't want to frighten her, but he knew he had to wake her. He had to know where she was going and secretly hoped it was the same direction he was going.

He stepped forward. "Miss," he said gently. When she didn't stir, he reached out and touched her shoulder. "Miss," he said again. This time she sat straight up and stared at him in disbelief.

"I'm sorry to disturb you, Ma'am, but this is where the trains change. Unless this is your final destination," Milo said.

"*Oh!*" she yelped, clutching her chest. "Umm, thank you."

"I'm sorry to have startled you," Milo said before making his way off the train. He tucked himself between the train cars and watched the young miss as she proceeded to the next train. He smiled in spite of himself, pleased to know that for now, she was at least traveling west.

CHAPTER 6

Kitty walked along the platform, looking for her next train, her heart still racing. She was certainly alert now. Since the man disembarked the previous train before her, she hadn't seen which direction he'd gone and that left her with an uneasy feeling she couldn't shake. If only she knew the man's name.

As she neared her next train, she noticed an older woman guiding a younger woman toward the train. Kitty could feel the fear radiating off the younger lady in heavy waves. Her face was badly bruised, and she was trying to hide it from prying eyes with the shawl she wore over her head. She walked slowly as if every step she took required great effort, while holding tightly to the tiny bundle in her arms.

"You're almost there, Shannon. Once you get on that train, you can rest," Kitty overheard the older woman say as she stepped forward to offer her assistance.

"Excuse me, I'm boarding the same train, would you like some help?"

The young woman's eyes darted upward and then bounced between the lady she was with and Kitty. She was visibly shaking and the small bundle in her arms let out a little whimper.

"I'm sorry, I didn't mean to frighten you. I'd be glad to help," Kitty said.

"That would be most kind of you, dear. I'm not boarding the train with Shannon, it would be good for her to have a friend along the way. Where are you traveling to?" asked the older woman.

"Oregon, my sister lives out there and was recently married," Kitty said.

"Oh, how lovely. Shannon is going to Oregon, too."

Shannon remained quiet, looking at the ground and not speaking for herself. Kitty didn't know what had happened to the woman, but she was shaking uncontrollably, clinging to the bundle in her arms as if it were her lifeline. She was running from someone or something–and she was so young, too. Probably younger than Abby. Kitty's heart went out to her.

"Shannon," she spoke gently. "My name is Kitty. Would you like to be my traveling companion? I could help you with the baby," she offered.

Shannon looked to her companion and then ever so slightly nodded. It was then that Kitty noticed the bruising along her jawline, the busted-up lip, and the stitches above her eye. The area around her eye was multi-colored and swollen. Her lightly colored hair looked as if it hadn't been washed in a few days, and Kitty imagined there were more bruises she couldn't see.

"Would you like me to carry your bag?" Kitty asked and, again, the young woman nodded ever so gently.

Kitty reached down and picked up the bag, then walked with Shannon and her companion. When they reached the train, Kitty noticed Shannon's shaking increase. The woman assisting Shannon stopped and carefully took her by the shoulders.

"Shannon, you listen to me now. He's not here, he doesn't know where you are or where you're going. You get on that train with this kind lady and don't you dare come back. You know what he'll do if he finds out that wee babe is a girl, and you may not survive his next round of punishment."

Kitty found the woman's words riveting. What had happened to Shannon? The older woman peeled back the top part of the blanket Shannon was holding and placed a soft kiss on the baby's head.

"I will miss you both, but I'd rather you be safe than here," she said and then looked to Kitty. "Thank you for helping."

"It will be my pleasure." Kitty grinned and then helped Shannon onto the train.

* * *

MILO HELD BACK, blending into the shadows, but he overheard bits and pieces of the conversation. It looked like they were all headed to Oregon, but what really caught his attention was the name Shannon. He couldn't tell what she looked like or if she matched the description Detective Gibson had given him a couple years back, but he had to find out.

He waited until both women had boarded the train and gave it a few more minutes to ensure they were seated. This time, he wasn't hiding in the back. He'd sit as close to the women as he possibly could, hoping to gain information on who this Shannon was. It would be a miracle if she were Detective Gibson's niece. He just needed her last name for confirmation. Of course, he had the portrait, but even from where he'd been standing he could tell she was badly beaten.

He took his time boarding, the train looking ahead at nowhere in particular until he noticed the women out of the corner of his eye. They'd chosen to sit near the back, and the seat across from them happened to be empty. The sight of Kitty holding a baby in her arms did something funny to his insides, and he knew she'd noticed him as he took his seat. She raised her eyebrow, giving him a suspicious look.

Milo held back the smile that threatened to appear. It seemed Miss Kitty wasn't as fragile as she'd appeared earlier, but then one never got between a mamma bear and her cub. He knew the baby didn't belong to Kitty but the passion to protect them rolled off of her in fiery hot blaze. No, Miss Kitty was not one to be trifled with.

CHAPTER 7

itty glared at the stranger. He made her uncomfortable for some reason. She knew she was being irrational thinking that he was following her, but she couldn't help it. She knew how to handle anger, but not the feelings he was causing her. If she weren't holding Shannon's sweet baby, she'd reach over there and knock that smirk right off the man's face. That would make him think twice about staring, after all, it was rude. He was bound to make Shannon even more uncomfortable; the poor girl was terror-stricken as it was.

Turning away from the handsome, annoying stranger, Kitty ran her finger along the baby's soft cheek, thankful for the distraction. She couldn't imagine riding the train alone with that man. There's no telling what would happen. He made her feel things that she didn't understand.

"Shannon," Kitty looked up from the baby, "what is her name?" she asked.

"Emery Grace," Shannon whispered.

"That's a beautiful name," Kitty said.

"I named her after my mother. Her name was Grace. She died some time ago. I'm glad she's not here to see me now, though," Shannon said as her eyes filled with unshed tears. Kitty's heart broke for her a little more.

"If you don't mind me asking, how old are you…and what happened?" asked Kitty.

"Seventeen. After momma passed on Pa remarried. She was a mean woman. Then my pa died in a strange accident and she sold me. Eugene, the man who came to collect me, was supposed to take me to a saloon, but decided he wanted to keep me as his wife instead. At first, he was sweet to me and made me feel safe, but then he would go out drinking or something would go wrong at work. He turned mean real quick," Shannon said as she touched her swollen lip.

Kitty gasped. "Was-was the woman's name Natalie?"

"Yes, h-how did you know that?" asked Shannon.

"She married my papa too, and she tried to sell my sister and me," Kitty said.

"You got away? D-did your pa die, too?"

"Yes, unfortunately, he did. I buried my papa before leaving Atlanta. He'd been sick before he married Natalie but he got worse soon after. There is suspicion of poisoning. Natalie was arrested. Did you ever meet a man by the name of Bloomberg?" Kitty asked and glanced up at the stranger, giving him a scowl. She'd find out his name and heaven help him if he was Mr. Bloomberg.

* * *

MILO LISTENED as the two women talked, and his interest piqued tenfold when Kitty asked about Bloomberg. Shannon was about the right age to be Detective Gibson's niece, but he couldn't remember Gibson's sister's name. He needed to send a telegram to Gibson, but the idea of letting these two women out of his sight for even a brief moment held no appeal.

If Shannon was indeed Gibson's niece and Milo lost her, he'd never forgive himself. The good detective had been searching high and low for her for the past two years. No one knew what happened to her; one day she was there and the next she was gone. Same as Natalie. When the report from Miss Johnson of Colorado circled through, the detective went on high alert.

Milo couldn't blame him. He knew what it was like to live day in and day out knowing that he had failed to protect those closest to you. Alessa had only been sixteen when she'd disappeared. He'd been out with the Sheriff's posse, tracking the Miller boys, and when he returned, she was gone. He was supposed to protect her, and he couldn't even do that as a local deputy. He left his position and became a bounty hunter, leaving no stone unturned in his search for his sister.

He asked about her in every town he visited. Showed her picture to half a million people. He was beginning to think he'd never know what happened to her. Then a young girl from the saloon from where Miss Johnson escaped recognized Alessa from the photo. She had died protecting some of the girls from one of Bloomberg's rampages—a defender until the very end. Milo couldn't have been prouder of her, but he blamed himself every day for her death.

Milo turned in his seat to where he could face both women. He might not be able to hear as well this way, but he had learned to read lips some time ago. When he looked up, they were both watching him intently. He didn't know whether to be alarmed or pleased. Why were they looking at him, he'd done nothing to draw their attention?

He heard Shannon say, "No, that's not him." What had

Kitty asked? How did he miss it? He watched as Kitty's ripe strawberry lips parted and she flashed him a wicked grin as if she knew something he didn't. Milo had a sinking suspicion he was now in trouble. Two women plotting against one man never went well.

CHAPTER 8

As the train crossed into Oregon, Kitty realized Shannon and Emery Grace were not going to Silverpines with her. They'd grown close along their journey west, with Kitty treating Shannon's injuries and helping tend to Emery Grace. She hated to see them go.

"Shannon are you sure you can manage? Perhaps I should get off in Sisters with you and see you safely to—where did you say you were going?" Kitty asked.

"Grace Landing," Shannon whispered. "You can't tell anyone. If my husband or Mr. Bloomberg ever found it, a lot of women would be in grave danger. It is a secret that very few are privy to.

"I would feel better if I saw you safely there. It will be difficult for you to travel alone, injured as you are, with Emery," Kitty said.

"If you insist, but your sister is going to be mighty upset you're late." Shannon smiled.

"Abby will understand, and she would expect me to make sure you and little Emery are safe," Kitty said. "Sisters isn't all that far from Silverpines, it won't take me but a day's train ride once we get you settled in."

Kitty watched the landscape rise and fall. Each smoky peak reaching higher than the last, as if competing against one another. Together they lay like slumbering giants beneath a blanket of thick pines, dominating a pale blue horizon with their glistening crowns of white, clashing against powdery puffs of cloud. Grassy plains bathed in wildflowers lay at their feet, while sparkling streams wove through, reflecting the jagged peaks within her mirror. It was as if Oregon herself was announcing her wonderous splendor.

In that moment, Kitty found herself thankful for the pioneers that had gone before her, discovering the magnificent beauty. She'd heard the stories of the Oregon Trail, even her papa had told her what a grand adventure it would be, that she would witness landscapes others only dreamed of. She wondered what Abby thought of living in such a luscious land. It was vastly different from Atlanta.

"Shannon, what is your husband's surname?" Kitty asked and when her question went unanswered, she turned to see Shannon had dozed off, the sun bathing her in a warm light.

While Kitty admitted she had a temper, she'd never been prone to violence. However, her thoughts toward the man that had harmed Shannon were none too kind.

* * *

"Next stop, Sisters," The conductor called out. Milo stirred from his position. He'd pretended to be asleep for the last hour or so but the moment he moved he sensed Kitty's eyes upon him. She was certainly an observant one and he'd have to be careful trailing her now.

He didn't want to give Detective Gibson false hope, yet

his gut said this was the right Shannon. He supposed he could just ask her. However, if she didn't want her own mother to see her, God rest her soul, she probably didn't want her uncle to, either. Milo couldn't risk her denying her identity, there were far too many similarities in her story for Milo to ignore it.

Milo watched the ladies beneath the brim of his hat as Kitty helped Shannon gather her things to disembark. If he were quick he might be able to send his telegram and still trail the women as he had not heard Shannon's whispered destination.

He stood, brushing against Kitty's arm in the process. An unexpected jolt of electricity shot through him and he took a quick step back.

"Sorry, Ma'am, didn't mean to bump you," he said, the words stuck in his throat as if he'd swallowed a bit of cotton fluff. Why did she extract such a response from him? He'd enjoyed the little look-sees she'd given him and listening to her voice as she conversed with Shannon, but he never expected her to elicit such a reaction. It was further evidence that he needed to steer clear of the young *bella signorina*, though his gut said she would be the one to lead him to Bloomberg.

Her eyes bore into him now as she moved to Shannon's side protectively. He hadn't meant to ruffle her feathers, but the fiery little mite looked as though she might take his head off if he came any closer. Her movement, however, allowed him to escape the confines of his seat. "Pardon me, Ma'am." He tipped his hat and rushed off the train in search of the telegraph office, the sound of laughter echoing in his ear.

"Kitty, I think you frightened that poor man." Shannon laughed, and Kitty smiled at the pleasing sound of it as the exited the train.

"I was tired of him staring at me as if I were his next

dinner. He might not be Mr. Bloomberg, as you say, but I believe he is following me for some reason. Why else would he be here?"

"Perhaps, he has business or family here. I don't know, did you think to ask him?" Shannon teased.

"Well no," Kitty sputtered. "Why would I do such a thing?" she asked, startling Emery awake in the process.

"To get your answers, silly. I think you like him, and I think he is enamored with you," Shannon said as she soothed the baby, who now looked around her surroundings with bright eyes.

"Did you see how fast he ran off this train?" Kitty asked, not willing to admit her attraction to the man.

"Yes, you frightened him." Shannon giggled, "besides he's not a bad man. I know bad men. He seemed more like some kind of lawman to me."

"Me? Frighten a big, tall man like that?" Kitty shook her head, blushing.

Laughter bubbled up in Shannon and poured over, causing her to stop and catch her breath. "Kitty, don't make me laugh, my ribs are still sore." She smiled.

"Well, he's gone now, anyway." She pouted. "So, how do we get to Grace Landing?"

"With them." Shannon pointed toward two women wearing trousers, both with guns at their hips.

"How do you know?" marveled Kitty.

"I was told who to look for. One tall blonde and one tall with black hair. Come on, I have to tell them who I am, but more importantly who you are. They are only expecting Emery and I," Shannon explained as they approached the two women.

"Hello, my name is Shannon Crowley, and this is—"

"Crowley?" interrupted Kitty. "I asked earlier, but you'd fallen asleep. Shannon, what was your husband's full name?"

"Eugene Crowley the third. He—he works for Mr. Bloomberg," whispered Shannon, while looking at the ground.

Reaching out her hand she placed it on Shannon's arm causing her to look up. "Shannon, a man by the name Crowley was shot and killed in Atlanta—when he came to collect Abby and me."

"You mean—he—he's gone?" sputtered Shannon.

"That's enough information for me," interjected the tall blonde woman. "How about you ladies load up and discuss this in the back of the wagon. My name is Frances, and this, is Alice. We'll take you to the valley."

"Thank you. My name is Kitty. I've been helping Shannon along the trip. I appreciate you letting me come along."

The two women nodded, and she climbed into the back with Shannon. "I'm sorry, I didn't know," apologized Kitty.

"Please do not apologize. You've nothing to be sorry for. Unknowingly, you've saved me from years of hiding. The only person I have to ever worry about now is Mr. Bloomberg. If he is ever caught, I just might have a chance at true love someday, Kitty. Something you should think about if you ever see that man from the train again."

"I—I don't know Shannon. When you love people, well in my case, they always leave."

The wagon was turning toward the mountains and continued drawing closer until Kitty feared they would run into them. Instead, the woman expertly lead them through the mountain and, hidden between the smoky peaks, the blanket of pines gave way to a secluded valley. A large looming structure greeted you at the valley's entrance. Women sat like sentries among the many rocking chairs with rifles draped across their laps and gun belts strapped to their hips. Obviously, one did not enter the valley without going through them first.

Once granted access, the building served as a holding place and hospital until each injured woman that arrived was well enough to be on her own. She would then be moved to one of the tiny homes that dotted the valley floor beyond main house. There she would work with the other women to survive and overcome the fears life had thrust upon them. Grace Landing was a place where they would learn to feel safe once again. The change in Shannon appeared to have happened overnight, though two weeks had passed. Kitty realized Grace Landing was the best place Shannon could have ever landed.

She also knew it was time for her to go. Abby would be worried by now, but the women had so many needs that it was difficult to turn away. They had all suffered at the hand of Mr. Bloomberg, or men just like him. No men lived in the valley. Only the same two men brought supplies from time to time, never going past the main house. The benefactor came once a year but, otherwise, left the women to it, and they were thriving. The women had big plans and Kitty longed to watch them unfold, or help in some way. For that she had an idea, but she would need to discuss it with Abby first.

"You take care of Emery," Kitty said, softly kissing the baby's head. "And write to me regularly. I'll visit as often as I can."

"I know you will, and I thank you for that, but Kitty, Abby's waiting for you. Go see her, make sure she, too, is safe and bring her to visit. I'd like to meet her," Shannon replied.

"I'll return soon," Kitty said, hugging Shannon tightly, then climbed on the back of Alice's horse and left the sacred valley.

CHAPTER 9

*S*ilverpines, Oregon June 1899

MILO COULD HAVE KICKED HIMSELF. How had two women disappeared from a train so quickly. He hadn't been gone that long, and yet, when he returned they were nowhere to be found. He searched the small town of Sisters, checking every nook and cranny he could find. He even asked about the women at the livery. No one had seen them or if they had, they weren't talking. Some bounty hunter he was. He couldn't even keep track of two women and a baby.

Dragging his long legs down the dusty road, he headed to the train depot once again. His movements slow and painful as each of his failures stacked another stone upon his six-foot six-inch frame. His posture sagged with the weight of it all. How could he have lost them? Where there was hope before, now sat a mountain upon his chest making it difficult to fill his lungs with air.

At least he knew where Kitty was headed. What he

couldn't understand is why she hadn't arrived yet. After all, Abby was getting married today. He'd been in Silverpines for two weeks already, with no sign of Kitty or Bloomberg.

Kitty should be here, he thought as his mind wondered. Was she hurt? Had she changed her mind? What had caused her delay? He'd give it one more day and, if Miss Kitty didn't show, forget Bloomberg, he was going in search of that fiery little woman.

Milo leaned against the depot wall and settled in to wait for the train, again.

* * *

Kitty sat rigid in her seat as the train approached Silverpines. Shannon had given her a detailed description of Mr. Bloomberg and Kitty found herself sitting directly across from him. Her back and shoulders ached from her stiff posture.

She held tight to the derringer tucked into the hidden pocket of her skirt, though she still wasn't a very good shot with it. The women at Grace Landing had taught her to shoot a rifle, but she couldn't seem to hit what she was aiming at.

Mr. Bloomberg looked nothing like the handsome stranger she had thought was following her earlier in her journey. He'd run off the train in Sisters like his britches were on fire, and Kitty hadn't seen him since. Not that it really mattered, she wouldn't be opposed to the tall stranger following her, now that the object of her nightmares was sitting across from her.

Kitty watched Mr. Bloomberg from beneath her lashes. If he knew who she was, he made no indication of it. But what if he had Abby's description and knew where she was? Why else would he be going to Silverpines? She had to get to Abby before he did. She had a promise to keep and she wouldn't be breaking it anytime soon.

"Next stop, folks, Silverpines," the conductor called out. Kitty gathered her items without taking her eye off Bloomberg. If she could get off the train before him, she'd have a head start, which she needed as his legs were much longer than hers. Kitty realized she had one thing in her favor that perhaps he didn't. Bloomberg might know Abby was in Silverpines, but that didn't mean he knew where to find her.

Abby had fled Atlanta to marry Reverend Bates, so the most logical place to find her would be the church or a house next to it. She could only pray she was correct. The train crawled to a stop and Kitty stood. Bloomberg remained seated, so Kitty darted into the aisleway, anxious to get as far away from the man as quickly as possible. She had to find out where the church was.

"Silverpines!" the conductor called out and, a moment later, the train door opened. Kitty rushed off the train and ran up to the first person she saw standing on the platform.

"Excuse me, can you tell me where the church is?" she asked.

"Sure thing, missy. Take a left on Third Street there and a right on Birch. Church is just past the park, ya can't miss it. Ya here for the weddin'?" he asked.

"Yes, yes. Thank you!" Kitty called out as she sprinted down the road he indicated. Right past the handsome stranger, but she didn't have the time to slow down and figure that out. She had to get to the church, to Abby. She knew of no other reason that devil of a man would be in Silverpines.

Kitty paused to catch her breath and looked behind her; Bloomberg wasn't there. She leaned down to take off her shoes because she could run better barefoot. Shoes in hand, she set out again and watched in horror as Bloomberg cut across the park to the church. How had he gotten ahead of her? She ran after him with renewed energy. He would not harm Abby.

As he flung the doors open, Kitty ran past. "Abby!"

"Kitty!"

"Why are you in a wedding dress? Aren't you already married?" Kitty looked to the man who stood frozen at her sister's side staring down the aisle at Bloomberg.

"Yes, Kitty, I'm married. You just missed the ceremony," she said as she pulled her husband closer.

"B-but, I–I don't understand," Kitty stammered.

"Well, you are a little late in arriving. I'll explain it later—"

"I want that man arrested for murder!" shouted Mr. Bloomberg as he pointed at Abby's new husband.

"Kitty, wh-who is that man and what is he talking about?" asked Abby.

"And for theft of property," he pointed right at Abby. "That is rightfully mine," he shouted as he marched toward them

"Natalie's real husband," Kitty stated flatly. Abby's brow furrowed, and her mouth formed into an O, but no words came out.

"I do believe his name is Douglas Bloomberg, isn't that correct Akecheta?" asked a man wearing a star on his chest.

Kitty watched as Abby's husband stood mute. Kitty spoke up, "Yes, that is Douglas Bloomberg. He attempted to purchase Abby and I, though neither of us have ever been for sale."

"I do believe, Mr. Bloomberg, that it is you I shall be placing under Federal arrest for violating sections one and two of the thirteenth amendment to the Bill of Rights, for buying and/or selling a person into involuntary servitude. By the way, we've been expecting you. Now, y'all get back to the festivities and I'll escort this fella down to the jailhouse. Mr. De Luca has been here waiting on him. I'll be back in a jiffy," he said. As he exited the church Kitty heard him say, "Well, Mr. De Luca, fancy seeing you here."

She turned to Abby. "Who is Mr. De Luca?"

"I haven't met him personally, but the rumor around town is, he's the tallest man alive."

Outside the church, the Marshall tipped his hat to Milo. "Mr. De Luca."

"Marshal."

"I'm pleased to see your warning panned out. I was starting to think this here fella wasn't gonna show," said Marshal Sewell.

"You and me both, Marshal."

"You know, De Luca, I can't leave town and haul him down south to the state penitentiary. I haven't got any deputies to watch over the town. I won't leave these women unprotected, they've been through enough, but I'll make a deal with ya."

"Yeah, what's that?"

"I got one of them Gardner shackles at the jail house. You haul him down to Salem for me and the bounty is yours, free and clear."

"You can't put one of those on me!" shouted Bloomberg.

"It'd be my pleasure." Grinned Milo. "I've been chasing this pond scum far too long."

"One other thing…" said the Marshal.

"Yeah?"

"I'm hurting for some deputies around here. I could sure use an honest man with your abilities. You think about it. If I see your mug back in town, I'll assume you want the job."

"I just might take you up on that, Marshal," said Milo.

"Thought ya might."

* * *

KITTY MET the eccentric Miss Edie and Miss Ethel during Abby's wedding reception in the park. She'd met so many women. Miss Edie introduced her to Ella Grace and Michael Karson, owner of the Silverpines Inn, and suggested she stay there for a time, as the newlyweds needed their special time alone to get acquainted. Though Kitty had wanted to be with Abby, she understood and accepted the room. She knew things would be different with Abby married.

Now, two weeks later, she sat in the dining room of the inn at her favorite corner table, sipping a cup of hot coffee. Most women preferred tea, but Kitty found she liked the stronger flavor. She unfolded the newspaper and scanned it for property ads, wondering how soon she could find a place of her own.

Her intended, Mr. Black, had died in the destruction that hit the town and, with the town in the process of rebuilding and recovering, Kitty feared any home she might find to purchase would need repair. Repairs she didn't know how to take care of on her own, and the last thing Kitty wanted to be was a burden.

With as few townsmen as there were, she knew she couldn't ask them for assistance. She had the funds to remain at the inn as long as she needed, that wasn't the problem. Kitty longed for her own space and her own home.

Perhaps if she had a place of her own to tend to, the boredom that threatened to overtake her would evaporate. Kitty had never been one for sitting still, maybe she could find a job to occupy her time. The she thought prodded her as she sat flipping the paper. Ella Grace approached with the coffee pot. "Would you like a refill, Kitty?"

"Thank you, that would be lovely. I'm not used to this cool mountain air yet," she said as an advertisement fell from the newspaper to the floor. Ella Grace leaned down to pick it up. "The Grooms Gazette? Are you going to put an ad in, too?" she asked, excitedly.

"An ad for what?" asked Kitty, raising her eyebrow in confusion.

"A husband, silly." Ella Grace replied with a small giggle.

"What on earth would I do that for?"

"It's how I met my Michael. I put an ad in for an innkeeper. Betsy started it by sending off for a marshal, and then several of us followed suit. Millie wanted a shopkeeper, and Sarah a gunsmith. Even Abby placed an ad for a preacher."

"She did not." Kitty looked at Ella Grace, flabbergasted.

"You really should talk to your sister a bit more, Kitty." Ella Grace winked. "The town needed a new preacher after Reverend Bates passed on, and Abby needed a protector. The town was littered with conmen and it wasn't safe for Abby to be alone as she was. So, Betsy spoke with her and Abby placed an ad for a preacher. There was a bit of a fiasco, though, when multiple preachers arrived to marry her, not having corresponded with Abby at all. She was furious."

Kitty sunk back into her chair, shocked by what Ella Grace had told her. "I do need to talk to my sister. Goodness gracious. I certainly did not have the whole story. So, the women of this town placed ads asking for men according to what the town needed?" Kitty questioned.

"More or less. We still have many needs, the most pressing being a few deputies to help the Marshal out. Betsy's expecting a baby anytime now, you know. Marshal Sewell is even threatening to hire women, you could send for a deputy and save him some trouble," Ella Grace suggested with a sly grin. "You think about it." She turned to check on the other patrons in the dining room.

Trouble, Kitty thought. That's just what a husband would

be. However, if the Marshal were willing to have a female deputy, it would help the town and keep her from going stir crazy. She looked down at the Grooms Gazette, shaking her head. Nope, she didn't need a husband. Kitty had no desire to live under a man's thumb or run the risk of dying while bringing his child into the world. She'd narrowly missed matrimony the first go around, she wasn't about to try it again. Not even for the tall, black haired, dark eyed stranger that followed her night after night in her dreams. *Who was that man?*

She downed the last of her coffee. It was time to take care of business and clear the fog from her head brought on by the handsome man. Standing, she decided she was going to be the town's new deputy, and that meant an overdue visit with Betsy, the marshal's wife.

CHAPTER 10

Kitty sat at the café, enjoying one of Lily Jo's lemon and blueberry scones while she waited for Abby to arrive. She couldn't wait to share her new plan with Abby. Betsy was completely on board. All Kitty had to do now was convince Marshal Sewell and order a few more riding skirts from the mercantile. She had some britches she could wear, but worried the town might frown upon it, that and she knew a female deputy wasn't what some people would want.

The young café owner, Lily Jo, seemed distracted and nothing at all like the bubbly person Kitty had been led to believe she was. Kitty watched as the young woman worried with her apron strings, fiddled with the tea bags, rearranged the tea cups, and continuously running up the stairs for something. This couldn't be *the* Lily Jo, everyone talked about, could it?

The bell above the door rang out, pulling her from her musings as Abby walked in, the wind propelling her forward as she pushed the door closed behind her.

"Morning Kitty, Lily Jo." Abby said as she removed her

scarf and unbuttoned her jacket, hanging it over the back of the chair. "It's brisk out there this morning." Abby took her seat across from Kitty. "You been here long?" she asked.

"Long enough to watch your little friend there run up and down the back stairs about five times." Kitty nodded her head in Lily Jo's direction.

"Umm…" Abby said as watched Lily Jo approach.

"Morning Abby, what can I get you?" She asked, sounding as if all the cheer in the world had been sucked right out of her.

"I think the better question, Lily Jo," Abby reached out and took her hand, "is what's wrong? What can we do to help?" asked Abby.

"My pa." Lily Jo sniffled and wiped her eyes. "He's taken a turn for the worse. The fever won't stay down, and he moans out as if he's in a terrible pain. I don't know what else to do for him. He's not making much sense."

"Have you gone for Hattie or Dr. Childs yet this morning?" asked Abby.

"I was trying to keep him comfortable while waiting for Hattie to come in for her tea. She usually does once or twice a day," she said, shuffling her feet and looking toward the stairs.

"Lily Jo, I think you need a bit of fresh air. Step away from this for a moment. Why don't you put your coat on, then run and fetch Hattie? Kitty and I will mind the café and tend to your pa," said Abby.

"A-are you sure that's alright?" asked Lily Jo as she wiped her eyes with the edge of her apron.

"Go, we'll be fine here," Abby said, ushering Lily Jo out the door and turning back to Kitty. "That poor girl, she just turned seventeen and she's been running this place on her own since the quakes. Her pa was injured and hasn't recovered. Lately, he's been slipping in and out of consciousness.

I'll go check on him and be right back. I'm not sure there is much I can do at this point."

Kitty smiled. "Papa was right, you were meant to be a pastor's wife."

* * *

LILY JO RETURNED to the café with Hattie, flipping the closed sign as they entered.

"Morning Abby, Kitty," said Hattie. "How about you assist me upstairs with Mr. Thompson?" she suggested, and the three of them followed Lily Jo up the stairs.

Buck Thompson lay in a large four poster bed in the bedroom at the top of the stairs. The room was dimly lit with the curtains pulled. The smell of sickness and death loomed. The sight immediately conjured memories of Papa's last days. Kitty and Abby stood back and looked on mournfully.

"Pa," Lily Jo whispered. "Pa, Miss Hattie is here to see you." Tears flowed down her rosy cheeks as she stepped back to allow Hattie to work. Abby stepped forward, taking Lily Jo's hand in hers. Kitty stood silently, watching the scene before her with an all too familiar feeling.

Buck Thompson made no response. Even from where Kitty was standing she could tell his breathing was shallow and his time limited. Hattie listened to his heart and lungs and checked his pulse before turning to Lily Jo.

Kitty stepped forward then, taking Lily Jo's other hand in hers. No young lady should ever have to go through this alone, she thought, remembering her own papa's passing.

"Lily Jo," Hattie said softly. "Your pa's body is tired of fighting the infection. He's too weak. His heart can barely keep up, and he's slipped into a coma. I'm so sorry. I wish there was something more I could do for him. He's fought hard for you, Lily Jo; his body is just giving out on him."

Lily Jo nodded.

"I'll go for Pastor James. Abby will stay with you." Kitty said as she squeezed Lily Jo's hand and departed the room.

Abby helped guide Lily Jo into a nearby chair. "Here sweetheart, perhaps you should sit." Lily Jo said nothing, only stared at her pa as each tear that fell chased another one down her sweet face. "Abby, maybe you should pray while we wait on your husband," suggested Hattie.

Abby knelt on the floor, taking Mr. Thompson's hand in hers and turned to take Lily Jo's as well. "Heavenly Father, we come to you in this hour of need. We ask for a smooth passage for Mr. Thompson and healing for Lily Jo. Your Word tells us that you are close to the broken hearted and save those who are crushed in spirit. Hearts are breaking here today, Lord, and we need you in this very hour. In Jesus's name, Amen."

"Thank you," Lily Jo whispered, though it was barely heard above the sound of the bell downstairs alerting them to Kitty's return with Pastor James.

Kitty entered the room and went directly to Lily Jo's side. Pastor James followed with Mr. Kisling trailing him. Abby had teased Kitty, saying she could marry a pastor too, but Mr. Kisling was in love with Lily Jo, and she with him. Though neither had made a move toward courtship. Kitty assumed it wouldn't be long before they came to an agreement. If it hadn't been evident before, it was crystal clear now as he approached her.

Lily Jo never took her eyes off her pa as they sat there with her, praying and offering what little support they could. Mr. Thompson's breath became irregular and Lily Jo rushed to his side. "It's okay, Papa," she said, smoothing his brow. "I'll be alright. You can go now. Say hello to Mum for me. I love you." She laid her head upon his chest.

With Lily Jo's blessing, Mr. Thompson took one last deep breath and then departed from this earth.

* * *

MILO HAD DELIVERED Douglas Bloomberg to the penitentiary and spent the last few weeks feeling as if he were lost wandering among the wilderness. Bloomberg had been the driving force behind his career as a bounty hunter. Now that Bloomberg was accounted for, Milo didn't know if he had it in him to chase the bad guys across the country anymore. He was tired.

The offer to serve as deputy in Silverpines lingered in the back of his mind. It held promise. He wouldn't mind planting his roots and being a part of a community, but there lay the problem. He would be responsible for the safety of the town, the same town Kitty now called home. What if he failed? There was only one way to find out.

He drained his coffee, paid his tab, and walked out of the Salem diner. A train whistle blew in the distance as if calling him home, confirming Milo's decision. He approached the depot and purchased a ticket back to Silverpines. Back to Kitty.

CHAPTER 11

Kitty smiled as she leaned back in the chair, propping her boots up on the desk. This was the life. Marshal Sewell had begrudgingly given into her and Betsy's demands and hired her to be his deputy. She still didn't have a home to call her own, but she was no longer staying at the inn. When Lily Jo's pa passed on, Kitty had offered to stay with her.

The arrangement worked out well for the both of them. Kitty was able to make sure Lily Jo was eating and taking care of herself, as well as help out around the café when she wasn't on duty. She had a purpose again. Someone to look after and people to protect, though, she worried about Lily Jo. The loss of her pa had destroyed the vibrant, cheerful young woman.

Just like Kitty, Lily Jo needed a purpose again, and Kitty had an idea…

The door to the jail opened and Kitty looked up into the dark mysterious eyes that had been haunting her dreams for months. What was he doing here and where had he been?

"Can I help you?" she said.

The man looked around the small jail as if he couldn't possibly be in the right place, and Kitty fought to hold back that laughter threatening to spring forth. Not everyone knew of her new position, especially strangers that stalk young women. It was high time she knew his name and he had some explaining to do.

"Yes, this is the jail. No, Marshal Sewell isn't in right now. Is there something I can help you with mister?"

"I, umm, I need to speak to the Marshal. He offered me a deputy position here a few weeks ago," he said.

"Well, Mr. Whatever Your Name Is, that position has been filled."

"By who?" he asked.

"By me," she answered smugly. "Now, is there something else I can help you with?"

"Uh, no Ma'am, I guess not. Good day." He quickly turned and walked back out the door.

Kitty stood and stomped over to the window, planting her fists firmly into her sides. The nerve of that man, not giving her his name. A name she so badly wanted to know. Well, she wasn't having any of it; she was a deputy and that meant she had authority, and besides, it was plain rude not give a lady your name. It was time to make the rounds anyway, and she wanted to know who this stranger was, where he was staying and what he was doing in *her* town. Maybe he'd be at the inn and Ella Grace could get the man's name for her, otherwise she was going to have to make up something other than Mr. Dashing. She really couldn't call him that to his face.

* * *

MILO SHUFFLED his feet as he walked along in no particular direction. What had just happened and how was he supposed to protect Kitty if she were acting as deputy? Marshal Sewell must be out of his mind, deputizing a woman; women had no business being deputies. Especially this woman.

The marshal had told him the job was his if he wanted it. So, what had happened that made him hire Kitty? Milo shook his head as if to clear his thoughts and nearly fell over.

"Whoa there, De Luca. You been drinking?"

"Marshal?" Milo blinked away thoughts of Kitty.

"Are you alright there?" Marshal Sewell asked.

"Marshal, you know you got a woman down at the jail house claiming to be your deputy?" Milo asked.

"Ah, I see. You meet Miss O'Byrne, did ya?"

"Did you really hire her to be a deputy?"

"Here she comes. You make her mad or something?" Marshal Sewell asked cautiously, causing De Luca to turn around. Sure enough there she was, her coppery hair flying behind her, riding skirt flared out at her sides, and headed straight for him.

"Boy, if I was you, I think I'd run." Chuckled the Marshal.

"Afternoon Marshal, thank you for detaining my prisoner. I'm taking this man into custody," she said. "Hands behind your back Mr. No-name."

Milo stood there, slack jawed, unsure of what was happening, while she tied up his hands. He looked to the Marshal for help, but the ol' goat just stood there, arms across his chest, enjoying the show.

"Miss O'Byrne, you sure you can handle him?" asked Marshal Sewell. "He's got a good foot and a half on you."

"That means he falls down harder." She grinned sweetly as she pulled the rope tight. "Walk on Mr. No-name, and if you try anything funny, don't think I won't shoot," she threatened.

Milo took one last look at the Marshal and headed toward the jail house. This was not the welcome he'd expected. He'd only been back in town an hour. Why was this tiny slip of a woman arresting him, and what had he done to make her so angry? So much for asking her to dinner.

"Kick that door open, real nice like," Kitty said. Milo did as he was told and ducked down as he entered the jailhouse. "Take that open cell right in front of you." Milo walked in and she slammed the cell door closed behind him.

"Hey, what about my hands?" he asked.

"Turn around, put your hands against the bars," she said as she pulled a knife from her waistband. Again, he did as he was told, wondering if he'd lost is mind, putting his wrists out so close to that woman.

"Now then, I'm gonna be the one asking the questions, and if you don't tell me what I wanna know, I'm not letting you outta here until the Marshal says I gotta. Understand?"

"Yes Ma'am," Milo answered, unsure how else to proceed with the spitfire in charge.

"Why have you been following me? You were on the train from Sweetwater, then you boarded the train to Sisters, Oregon and sat across from me the whole way. Now, you show up here, where I live. Why have you been following me?" she asked.

"Ma'am, I was only traveling the same route as you. I'm a bounty hunter," Milo said.

"And just *who* were you hunting?" Kitty rolled her eyes.

"Douglas Bloomberg. Caught up to him here in Silverpines when the two of you interrupted the Pastor's wedding. Marshal Sewell had me haul the man down to Salem to stand trial for his crimes," Milo said.

"You weren't following me?"

"No, Ma'am, though I admit, I am interested in where Shannon went. I believe her to be the niece of my colleague, Detective Gibson," Milo said.

Kitty sat down and stared at him in disbelief just as the Marshal walked in.

"Did he answer all your questions deputy?"

"I got one more. What is your name?" Kitty asked

Milo grinned. "I'm kinda fond of Mr. No-name." Milo chuckled and looked toward the Marshal who threw his hands up in exasperation.

"Better tell her, especially if you're here for the job. Seeing as how you two would be partners."

"What!" they said in unison, leaving the good Marshal rolling in laughter.

"Just wait until I tell Betsy this one."

* * *

KITTY STORMED INTO THE CAFÉ. "The nerve of *that* man. I shoulda left him in there to rot!"

"What man, dear?" asked Fannie Pearl, the town matriarch.

"The one that followed me all the way here and now he wants my job, and he won't even tell me his name," Kitty huffed as she paced back and forth.

"He followed you?" Abby asked in alarm.

"He says he wasn't following me, but I think he's hiding something. How can I work with a secretive man that won't even tell me his name?"

"You questioned him?" Lily Jo asked.

"Oh, I did more than that, I arrested him."

"Oh, Kitty, you didn't. What would Papa say?" asked Abby.

"He'd tell me my Irish is showing, but Abby you don't understand. I would have left him in there if the Marshal hadn't told me to play nice," Kitty huffed.

"Well, Kitty dear, what's he look like?" Fannie Pearl asked. "I'm sure one of us can learn his name for you."

"Oh, nothing special really. He's a giant of a man with black hair, dark, brooding eyes, and a smooth jawline. Always wears dark clothes, a black hat, and stupid smirk on his face."

"Ya like him, don't ya?" Abby teased.

"Wh-what? No!" Kitty cried in irritation.

* * *

MILO AWOKE THE FOLLOWING MORNING, thankful for a good night's sleep. He was grateful to sleep in the room he'd reserved at the inn, versus the tiny jail cell Kitty had thrown him in, though, he had to admit he'd let her do it.

She sure was beautiful when she was angry.

He washed his face and dressed for the day. His stomach growled in response to the smells wafting up from the dining room. With all the excitement he'd forgotten to eat yesterday.

He headed downstairs and was greeted by Ella Grace who showed him to a table.

"Coffee?" she asked.

"Yes, please."

"Cream and sugar?"

"No, thank you. I like it black."

She poured his coffee, took his order, and then went on to see to her other guests. Milo gazed around the room at the people he would have to get to know, seeing as he was now one of the deputies serving Silverpines. It didn't go unnoticed that the majority of the town was made up of women, easy prey for con men and the like.

Ella Grace placed a plate of breakfast in front of him. "You enjoy that now," she said as she walked on toward an elderly woman who had entered the dining room. "Good morning, Fannie Pearl, it's nice to see you out."

"Thank you, Ella Grace. I'm meeting Abby and Lily Jo for breakfast."

"They haven't arrived just yet, but you can take a seat wherever you like."

"Thank you dear, those girls are never on time." Both women rolled their eyes in agreement.

Milo watched the older woman walk toward him, assuming she was taking the empty table in front of him. Until she sat down across from him.

"Hello there, I haven't seen you around these parts before. You trouble?" she asked.

Milo smiled. "No, Ma'am. The Marshal offered me a deputy position."

"That was mighty kind of him. We need a few good deputies around here. My name is Fannie Pearl, and everyone calls me Fannie Pearl. Don't you forget that now."

"No, Ma'am, I won't forget. I'm Milo De Luca, it's nice to meet you," he said, putting down his fork to take her hand.

"Likewise. Now, if you need anything you scurry on over and see me. I live just on the other side of the schoolhouse, and I know everyone in these parts, new and old. I make a point to as it's nice to know who your neighbors are."

"Yes, Ma'am. Thank you."

"My pleasure, Milo. Now, I best get a table before those girls come dragging in. It was nice visiting with you. Welcome to Silverpines," she said as she stood and went to an empty table in the middle of the room to wait for her friends.

Milo finished his breakfast and stood to leave as Fannie Pearl's friends arrived. He tipped his hat to her and made his way out the door. Thanking Ella Grace as he passed.

* * *

"OH MY, was that him, Fannie Pearl?" Abby asked in amazement.

"He's so tall. I don't believe I've ever seen a man quite that tall," said Lily Jo in awestruck wonder.

"Nor I," added Ella Grace. "I don't think we have a bed to fit his frame, but he didn't complain none. Would you ladies like coffee or tea this morning?"

"Coffee, Ella Grace. You know the way I like it," said Fannie Pearl.

"Tea for me," said Abby.

"Me too," added Lily Jo.

Ella Grace wandered off to get their drinks and Abby pounced. "Did ya get his name, Fannie Pearl?"

"Well, of course I did. Mr. Milo De Luca is our newest deputy. Y'all be nice to him. He's gonna have a hard enough time working with Kitty." Fannie Pearl snickered.

"I think she likes him," Abby announced with a sly grin.

"Me too." Lily Jo smiled.

"That's all well and good, but does our handsome new deputy fancy Kitty?" Asked Fannie Pearl.

"Don't tell her I said so," began Abby, "but I think she likes him much more than she'd like us to know. Rarely I have seen her blush as much as she did last night, when she was talking about arresting him."

"She did what?" Fannie Pearl buzzed with excitement.

"Yes, she arrested him and put him through the ringer. Pelted him with questions about why he was here and following her," Abby continued. "She was hopping mad when I saw her last night."

Lily Jo giggled. "Yeah, she could barely get her words straight other than to talk about how tall and dark he was."

CHAPTER 12

Kitty stood in the corner with her arms across her chest, and Milo sat in the chair on the other side of the room, neither speaking to the other. Marshal Sewell walked into the jail house to go over the duties with them.

"Y'all can't work together very well if you're gonna behave like toddlers throwing a temper tantrum," said Marshal Sewell.

"But…" Kitty started to speak.

"No buts, Miss O'Byrne. Here's how this is gonna go. You two are going out for some target practice and, when ya come back, I expect ya to be friends. If ya ain't, I'm gonna lock you both in a jail cell until you sort this business out between y'all. I need deputies I can count on and, right now, y'all are too busy shooting daggers at one another to be any help to me or this town. Now get going."

Kitty stomped out of the jail house, not even bothering to wait on Milo as she made her way to the livery. She was probably wondering why did he have to show up and ruin everything.

Milo followed behind Kitty, enjoying the sway of her hips. His long legs could have easily eaten up the distance between them, but he figured he was safer back here. Maybe this little exercise Marshal Sewell instructed them to do would help her blow off some steam, and he could talk to her. Milo knew he wouldn't be able to get to know her if she kept stomping off, throwing him in jail, or ignoring him every time he came near. If only he knew what he'd done to bother her so.

"Morning Jake, we need a couple horses," Kitty grumbled. "We won't be gone long."

"Sure, thing Miss O'Byrne," Jake said and went to retrieve their mounts while she waited.

He was gone only a moment and when he returned he handed her the reins. "Thanks, Jake," she said.

"If you don't mind me asking, you look a little down today. Anything I can do to help, Miss O'Byrne?" Jake asked.

"Only if you have a way to help me get rid of Mr. Irritating over there." Kitty pointed across the paddock to where Milo stood. "He has a way of getting under my skin like no one I've ever met. Now I have to go play nice with him."

Jake chuckled as Kitty left the stable with a long sigh.

Kitty thrust the reins of one of the horses into Milo's hand. She had no desire to work with this man. She didn't even want to be in the same area as him. He made her feel off balance and flustered, but she didn't know why. She felt a constant desire to either punch him or kiss him from the moment she saw him on the train.

Kitty led the way around the backside of the cemetery and up into the foothills to the shooting range Sarah had shown her. Kitty knew her aim wasn't that great, and it embarrassed her. She liked the privacy of the shooting range, but now she had to share it with him. She had to practice in front of someone—and not just any someone but *the* someone! Kitty wanted nothing more than to turn tail and run home.

She dismounted at the excavated hillside where the wooden targets were placed and turned to Milo. "These two horses are good with guns and they won't leave us stranded, so we can let them graze."

Milo nodded. "Uh, Miss O'Byrne?" he said carefully.

"Yes?"

"If the Marshal wants us to be friends and all, I reckon ya outta know my name."

"Well, I thought you liked Mr. No-name."

"I didn't mean to upset ya with that, you were just…" Milo sighed with resignation. "My name is Milo."

"I was *just what*, Milo?"

"Angry." He said as he sighted his revolver.

"Oh." She whispered as she removed her gun from the holster. It was heavier than the derringer she carried in her pocket, and she'd only shot it once since she purchased it from Sarah. Now, she was being forced to practice with *him*, instead of enjoying her shooting lessons with Sarah.

She watched him take his stance, positioning his long legs just so, as he aimed at the first wooden target. Kitty supposed he could shoot the targets on that side and she could shoot the others. Then she wouldn't be distracted by his presence. And if they were both shooting at the same time, perhaps he wouldn't notice her poor aim as much she feared.

Kitty stepped forward, still admiring Milo's long legs, and tripped over a large clump of mud. It sent her tumbling to the ground and she accidentally pulled the trigger in the process. She heard Milo's gun fire at the same time, and she prayed he didn't notice her blunder as she righted herself and stood back up.

"You shot me!" Milo yelled.

Kitty spun around to see Milo laying on the ground, gripping his backside. Good heavens, what had she done? How was she going to get that giant of a man back up?

"I—I, I didn't mean to." She ran to Milo's side, her gun left lying in the dirt. "I never meant—I…" Kitty couldn't stop the tears from pouring down her face. "I didn't…"

Milo reached up and tucked a strand of hair behind her ear. Then, using the pad of his thumb, he wiped her tears, one by one.

"God counts those, you know," he said, but she refused to look at him. "Kitty, look at me *bella signorina*." He tried again, this time placing his hand under her chin and lifting her head until her gaze met his. "I know you didn't mean to, but I'm gonna need to see the Doc," he said, looking into her golden eyes, and longing to kiss her sweet lips. "Kitty, you're gonna have to help me onto that horse."

"I— you—can't—Hattie's." Kitty sobbed.

"Kitty, get the horse," Milo urged, but she didn't budge. She was in a complete state of shock and he'd been shot. How had he got himself in this predicament? Milo groaned as he pulled his left leg forward and pushed up on his arms. Kitty remained seated next to him as sob after sob racked her small frame.

Milo could think of only one way to get her to snap out of it, and if she smacked him, at least she wouldn't be in shock anymore and could fetch the horse. He took a deep breath, placed his hands around her face, smoothed away a few more tears, and then—ever so lightly—touched his lips to hers. For a brief moment, nothing had ever felt more right in his world. Then her eyes widened, and she sat back.

"The horses," he said.

"Oh! Oh, you—you need Hattie," she said and sprinted as fast as her little legs would go toward the horses. Milo found himself smiling; at least she didn't smack me, he thought. It would be a pleasant memory to hang on to while the Doc dug the slug out of his backside. Of all the places she could have shot him, he thought. It brought new meaning to her getting under his skin. He winced as he tried to move into a better position.

"Here Kitty, give me the reins," he said as she approached. "I think if I hold on to them, I can pull myself up."

"H-how are you going to get on him, though?" She whimpered.

"I'm gonna lay across him and you guide us to, did you say, Hattie's?" Milo asked.

Kitty nodded and stood nearby as Milo pulled himself upright. His face had gone ghost white in the process. He stood there for only a moment before using his uninjured side to propel himself forward onto the horse's back.

She ran around to the other side of the horse. "Are you on there enough? Should I pull your arms forward some?"

He shook his head. "Hattie's." He groaned and promptly passed out.

CHAPTER 13

*L*ily Jo had been visiting with Pastor James about her grief. All the beautiful and heart-breaking memories were closing in on her, and she thought he might have some scripture to help her. She wasn't ready to discuss her feelings with her friends yet, unsure they'd understand her struggle.

She had always loved Silverpines and its people, but the tragedies had robbed Silverpines of so many. Lily Jo had lost her mum years earlier. She lost several of her friends in the earthquakes, the mine collapse, and later the mudslide. Now her pa was gone, and Lily Jo was struggling with her love for Silverpines. She'd lost everyone she had ever loved.

New people arrived, some good, some bad, and the rebuilding of Silverpines began. She watched as new love sprung forth among her remaining friends, as well as new life. Lily Jo was happy for them, but with Pa's passing, something had changed inside, and she was having a difficult time coming to terms with it.

She walked around the church to the cemetery, and sat down next to her pa's grave. "I don't know what I'm supposed to do now, Pa. I miss you." She wiped the tears from her eyes, then turned toward the sound of horses approaching, looking up to see Kitty's beautiful hair flying wild in the wind as she rode toward town. Following closely behind was a second horse. Something was wrong, Lily Jo could feel it.

She ran to the edge of the cemetery. "Kitty!" she called out. "Do you need help?"

"Need Hattie. Shot Milo," Kitty yelled back and kept going.

Lily Jo ran to the church, opening the front door. "Pastor James, we need help!"

Akecheta ran out of his study.

"Milo, the new deputy, has been shot. Come on!"

They ran toward Hattie's just as Kitty dismounted. "Lily Jo, can you get Hattie? Pastor James, he—Milo passed out. I— I don't know how to get him down," she cried.

Hattie and Dr. Childs came rushing out the door. "Pastor James, think you can help me get him off that horse and inside?" asked Dr. Childs. "On three—Hattie, get the door."

"I think he's taller than both of us, Doc," Akecheta said.

Kitty watched helplessly as the men lifted an ashen-faced Milo from the horse and carried him inside, laying him face down on an exam table that he was far too long for. His legs hung nearly completely off of it.

Hattie stepped forward. "Kitty, what's his name?"

"Mr. No-name—I mean, Milo," she said, wiping her tears with her sleeve.

"Lily Jo, can you sit with Kitty in the other room for right now, and Pastor James, can you please see to the horses?" asked Hattie.

Lily Jo took Kitty by the arm and guided her to the settee in the room Hattie had indicated.

"What happened, Kitty? Who shot him?"

"I—I did," Kitty cried, burying her face in her hands.

"Oh Kitty, I'm sure it was an accident," Lily Jo said, hugging Kitty to her.

* * *

HATTIE GATHERED the needed supplies for removing bullets while her husband cut away the deputy's britches. Once the material had been removed, Hattie set to cleaning the raw flesh. There didn't appear to be a great deal of blood loss.

"I know he's still out Hattie, but we may need a little dab of chloroform to make sure he doesn't wake while we remove this bullet. That's a small wound and I'm gonna have to dig around for the slug," said Robert while washing his hands.

She prepared a cloth with a small amount of chloroform; with Milo already out cold they had to be careful not to give him too much. She knew Robert was right, once he began looking for the bullet, the chance of Milo coming to was likely.

Hattie stood opposite of Robert, handing him the instruments he needed and keeping the area clean while he worked.

"Hattie, hold the skin tight there. I think I've got it, I don't want it to slip."

She watched as Robert carefully pulled the bullet from the tissue and dropped it in the pan with a metallic clink. Hattie didn't care much for bullet wounds. With a clean cloth, she wiped away the blood and applied pressure. Robert cleaned the instruments while she threaded a needle and began to sew up the raw, pink skin.

"I'll stay with him, if you want to see to Kitty," Robert said.

* * *

A PAIN THROBBING in his back side awoke Milo from his sleep. Where was he? What happened? He looked around the room, his eyes falling on the small, sleeping form in the nearby chair.

Kitty.

He smiled. Her hair had come loose and fallen down around her shoulders in large waves. He ached to run his fingers through it, to feel its soft texture and kiss her sweet lips.

She may have shot him, but he would never forget kissing her. It had been a quick decision to pull her from her shock, it lasted mere seconds. Would she welcome his kiss, he wondered? Milo tried to, carefully, move into a more comfortable position, but the pain became too intense. The throbbing intensified, and a grunt escaped Milo's lips, rousing his sleeping beauty.

"You're awake," she said, jumping from her seat. "Are you in pain? Do you need something? I'll get Hattie," she said, not waiting for an answer as she ran out the door in search of this mysterious Hattie he hadn't remembered meeting.

Kitty came rushing back into the room, dragging a young woman with long dark hair and dark eyes with her.

"Well, good afternoon Deputy, I'm Hattie Childs. How are you feeling?" she asked.

"A bit sore. How long have I been out?" he asked.

"You've been out a few hours, but we successfully removed the bullet from your backside," Hattie explained. "Now that you're awake, I'd like to check to make sure it is healing as it should. Kitty, would you mind leaving the room for a bit?"

Kitty nodded, looked at Milo with an apologetic smile, and closed the door as she departed.

Milo watched as Kitty left. "She been here the whole time?" he asked.

"She has. She feels awful, but now that she's stepped out, why don't you tell me how you're really feeling?" Hattie said.

"Perceptive, huh?"

"I've been doing this a long time." Hattie grinned.

"It's throbbing pretty good, feels a little warm—like ya must of have had to dig deep for that slug."

"I'll give you something for the pain. My husband *did* have to do some digging, but the wound itself was rather small," she said as she moved the sheet to check for bleeding or infection. "This looks to be clearing up nicely. We would like you to remain here a day or two, but then you should be able to move around. My husband has a cane you can use, though it may be a bit short. I'll also see if I can rustle up a few pillows, as sitting will not be a comfortable activity for a while."

"Thank you," Milo said.

"I'll let Kitty know she can come back in," Hattie said as she backed out the door.

* * *

LILY JO CLOSED the café and walked to Hattie's to check on Kitty and Milo. She knew Kitty was beating herself up over the accident, and wished there was something more she could do for her. How did one get over such a thing?

Stepping onto Hattie's porch, she heard Kitty asking a rather odd question and peered through the window.

"Hattie, if I were to place an ad for a husband, like Ella Grace suggested, would there be a way to prevent getting in a family way?" Kitty looked at her feet and scraped at the floor with her toe. Her cheeks burned red with embarrassment.

"Kitty, why wouldn't you want a baby?" Asked Hattie.

"Women die having babies, Hattie. My momma died having my brother, and Abby's momma, Lucy, died having her. I don't want to leave a baby without a momma. That's why I haven't pursued marriage. I also know I'm not a very good deputy, and Milo and Marshall Sewell should have someone they can depend on," Kitty said, quietly. Lily Jo thought, perhaps, there was more to this than what she was hearing through the open window.

"Yes, Kitty, some women die in childbirth, but we've come a long way since then, and you have me. Besides, you can't live life wondering things like that, Kitty. Wouldn't you rather be happy?" asked Hattie.

"I'm afraid to be happy. I'm afraid everyone will leave me, or I will leave them. Love hurts. I don't know if I'd make a good wife or live long enough to be a mother. I'm not a very good deputy. I have horrible aim. I—I shot Milo and—and he kissed me! Why did he kiss me?"

Lily Jo had heard enough, she needed to talk to Fannie Pearl and she needed to talk to her *now*. Lily Jo headed straight for the parsonage to find Abby, pleased that it was just across the street.

"Abby!" she hollered as she knocked. She heard Abby moving around and then the door opened.

"Why, Lily Jo, what a pleasant surprise."

"I would love to visit, but we have an emergency. We've got to go to Fannie Pearl's," she said, grabbing Abby's hand and pulling her outside.

"Whatever for?" Abby asked.

"I'll explain when we get there, but Fannie Pearl will know what to do. She always does."

"Alright, Lily Jo, let's go." Abby followed closely without any more questions.

"Thank you."

They rushed past Hattie's, the mayor's house, and across Main Street to Fannie Pearl's. Lily Jo knocked on the door and bounced on her toes while she impatiently waited for Fannie Pearl to open the door.

"What if she's not home, Lily Jo?" asked Abby.

"She's home. She's always home at this time of day, but we may be interrupting her nap."

"We could come back later…"

"No, we need her help," Lily Jo interrupted as she knocked again.

Fannie Pearl opened the door, rubbing her eyes. "Yes?" she asked before putting her glasses on. "Lily Jo, what's all this racket about?"

"I'm sorry, Fannie Pearl, but we need your help, it's of utmost importance," said Lily Jo.

"Well, come in, come in. Whatever is the matter?"

"That's what I've been asking," Abby exclaimed.

"Sit down, sit down, and tell me what's wrong."

"I went to visit with Kitty and see how Milo was doing, and I know I'm not supposed to eavesdrop, but the question Kitty asked Hattie shocked me. Kitty is talking about putting an ad in the paper for a husband, and for a new deputy. She thinks she is a terrible deputy since she shot Milo."

"But Kitty's afraid of getting married," Abby blurted.

"Kitty's afraid she'll have a baby and die like her momma and your momma, Abby. And—and *Milo* kissed her!"

Abby sat up straighter in disbelief. "Oh my goodness."

"Oh, that poor dear," said Fannie Pearl.

"I would have never guessed, Kitty loves babies. I knew she didn't want to get married but not why. She always said it was because she didn't want to be controlled by any man."

"Didn't you hear me?" Lily Jo stood. "She's going to send for a deputy *and* Milo kissed her!"

"I see the problem," said Fannie Pearl.

"You do?" Abby asked. "I don't."

"Abby dear, didn't you say Kitty liked Milo?"

"Yes, she did." Lily Jo bounced on her toes and clapped her hands.

"I—I guess I don't understand, Lily Jo," said Abby.

"We need to confiscate Kitty's ad and give it to Milo." Lily Jo bounced around the room.

"Oh, what a brilliant idea, Lily Jo," Fannie Pearl cried.

"How do we do it, Fannie Pearl?" Lily Jo asked. She was determined to help her friend and see to her happiness. Lily Jo loved helping others and giving to them. It brought her true joy.

"First, I'm going to go see Milo," conspired Fannie Pearl. "Lily Jo, you convince Kitty to write that ad quickly. Then, offer to send it off for her, but bring it to me instead. If Milo is truly interested, then Abby you will help him respond to Kitty's ad and, Lily Jo, you'll make sure she gets the response."

"This is so exciting. Thank you, Fannie Pearl." Lily Jo clapped, excitement coursing through her.

"It's been a while since I played matchmaker, but I think I still got it." Fannie Pearl smiled. "Now, you get Kitty to write that letter. I'm going visiting."

CHAPTER 14

Fannie Pearl dressed in her best go- visiting dress, attached her favorite brooch, and brushed her hair. After putting on her apron, she pulled the fresh biscotti from the oven and wrapped them in a dish. One never went visiting without a neighborly gift, and when one was on a particular matchmaking mission, a *sweet* was required.

She opened the door and stepped out into the cool autumn air. It was her favorite time of year and perfect for giving Cupid a little hand. If Paul were watching from above, he would be proud of her for helping these young ones find love. She watched the children play as she passed by the park, waving hello to neighbors she saw along the way to Hattie's.

Hattie was outside watering some plants when she walked up. "Afternoon Hattie, I came to visit with your patient and I brought treats."

"How sweet of you, Fannie Pearl. I'm sure Milo would enjoy the company. Kitty left not long ago, and I daresay the man has been pouting ever since."

"Now that sounds promising, doesn't it?" She winked at

Hattie and followed her inside to the room where Milo was recovering.

"Milo, I've brought you a visitor," said Hattie.

Fannie Pearl sat in the seat where Milo could see her. "So, how's the sore backside? She shot you in the tuchus, did she? You know, maybe that bullet was actually from Cupid. Seems to me like he might have had to use something a bit stronger to get your attention."

"Wait…Fannie Pearl, it was just an accident," Milo retorted.

"Of course, it was. Kitty couldn't hit the broad side of a barn, but yet she managed to get you."

"Yes, well, I've learned my lesson. I won't be target practicing with her again. I'm not sure she'll pick up another gun, anyway."

"You're not listening to me boy. You most definitely need to take her shooting again, but this time, you gotta put your arms around her to keep that bullet going straight. Who knows. Maybe when you hold her tight you just might break that wall she's been hiding behind. Rumor about the town is you two been sparking." Fannie Pearl leaned forward in her chair, making eye contact with Milo. "Of course, you might wanna tell ol' Fannie Pearl here otherwise? Which is it?"

"Ma'am?"

* * *

"Lily Jo, I have an idea," Abby said. "I ended up in Silverpines because my papa and Kitty wrote to Reverend Bates without telling me, and I couldn't be happier. At the time, I didn't know I was leaving Atlanta or getting married until the day Kitty put me on the train. I was scared to death. I think I owe my dear sister a favor." Abby grinned.

"So, you want to write the advertisement, instead of Kitty?"

"Yes, and I want you to give it to Milo. We're never going to mail it and we can give it to Kitty as a wedding gift. She'll thank us later."

"But what will Kitty say when she gets a response and what if she actually writes one?"

"For as upset as she is right now, if Kitty is considering placing an advertisement, she'll say yes. If she writes one, hide it from her, you do live together."

"Won't she be upset with you?"

"Maybe at first, but when she finds out it's Milo..." Kitty shrugged. "Trust me, I know my sister, and if she's willingly walking into marriage, it's gonna be with Milo."

"Well, let's write it. I'll deliver it to him at the inn tomorrow. Hattie said he'd get to leave her house in a day or two, so I bet he's out first thing tomorrow," said Lily Jo.

"For starters, she wants a deputy, good thing we've already got one." Abby laughed as she picked up her pencil and wrote *Wanted: Deputy* on a piece of parchment. "What about something like...

Wanted: Deputy
Woman of twenty-three seeks groom between the ages of twenty-five and thirty-five. Must be God-fearing, Compassionate, Patient, Forgiving, and good with a firearm. If interested, please send response to Kitty O'Byrne.

What do you think Lily Jo?"

"I think it sounds perfect, and I hope she doesn't shoot us next."

* * *

MILO DRESSED in the clothes Michael Karson brought over from his room at the inn for him. He was pleased Hattie was releasing him today, but he would miss Kitty's long visits. He feared he might not see her as often now that he was on the mend. He buttoned the last button of his shirt, Fannie Pearl's words playing over and over in his mind. Could Kitty be interested in him?

He'd overheard her private conversation with Hattie. Kitty was planning on turning in her badge for a wedding ring and that frightened her. Milo had a gut feeling that Kitty had trouble believing in herself. He would never ask her to give up being a deputy, if she didn't want to. With the town predominantly women, he knew they responded well to Kitty and liked having her on their side.

Milo was excited that she remembered the kiss, though she assumed he thought it was nothing. She couldn't have been more wrong. It was everything, and the one thing he couldn't stop thinking about doing again.

He opened the bedroom door and stepped out. Hattie greeted him with a warm smile. "Making a break for it, I see," she said.

"Yes, Ma'am. I've taken up enough of your time and space, but I thank you for your care. You and Doc can patch me up anytime. I don't think I've recovered quite as quickly before," he said.

"I'm glad we could help, but please try not to get shot again."

"Comes with the job, Ma'am," he said, tipped his hat, and made his way outside.

The air had turned cooler and the walk to the inn would be a bit painful. However, he was looking forward to being in his own space again. He cut across the park and headed straight there, knowing the little exertion would have him sweating by the time he arrived. He hoped Kitty would come see him.

He crossed Main Street and looked up at the inn. Lily Jo was sitting in one of the rockers on the porch.

"Are you waiting on Fannie Pearl this time?" he asked her.

"No sir, I'm waiting for you. I wanted to make sure you made it here alright, and to give you this note. I hope you'll do the right thing." She said and placed a piece of folded parchment in his hand, then ran off down the street.

First, Fannie Pearl's odd visit, and now Lily Jo's… What was going to happen next, he wondered, tucking the parchment into his pocket. He needed a cup of Ella Grace's strong coffee. He opened the door to the inn and stepped inside. Michael stepped around the counter and clasped him on the shoulder. "Welcome back, stranger."

"Nice to be back. Coffee still hot?" Milo asked.

"The coffee is always hot. Have a seat and I'll get you a cup."

Milo carefully sat in the first booth and Michael handed him a coffee not a moment later. It felt good to be back. The inn had the feeling of home. The same feeling he noticed in Sweetwater, where he first saw Kitty. She took his breath away.

He reached into his pocket, pulling out the note Lily Jo had given him. His heart pounded as he read the words. Kitty had placed the ad for a groom after all, but how had Lily Jo gotten a copy of it, he wondered.

"Man, you've gone a bit pale. Need some help to your room?" Michael asked.

"No, I—Michael, can I ask you about something?"

"Sure, what's eatin' ya?"

"You're not originally from Silverpines, are ya?"

"No, I'm not. I came here to marry Ella Grace," he said.

"Did Ella Grace put an ad in the *Groom's Gazette*?"

"Yes. Many of the women in town have. The men were killed in the quakes and accidents that followed, why?"

"Kitty's looking for a groom," he said, knowing he sounded like an injured pup. He handed the parchment to Michael. "This note was given to me this morning."

"You interested? I can get you some parchment to write a response. Then I'd give it to whoever gave you this note."

"Why not Kitty herself?"

"Well, Deputy, do you think Kitty herself would have had that delivered to you?"

"You have a point. I think I will take that bit of parchment, please."

Michael walked to the desk and back and laid the writing utensils down on the table in front of Milo. "Need help or just a refill?"

"Refill will do fine. Thanks." Milo thought about the words he would use to describe Kitty and began to write.

Wanted: Deputy
Man of twenty-nine seeks bride between the ages of eighteen and
twenty-eight.
Must be God-fearing, Courageous, Passionate, Kind, and lousy
with a firearm.
If interested, please arrive at the Silverpines Church tomorrow at
noon.

"Michael," Milo called out, gaining the other man's attention. "What's the fastest way to spread word around these parts about a shindig?"

"Two-words, Fannie Pearl. She lives just two blocks from here."

"Thank you, Michael."

CHAPTER 15

*M*ilo found the house and knocked on the front door, the piece of parchment tucked in his pocket. He'd go see Pastor James next.

"Milo, nice to see you up and about," Fannie Pearl said, opening the door. "Come in, come in. Make yourself comfortable."

"Thank you, Ma'am. I can't stay long, but I seem to recall being told if I ever needed anything to scurry on over here."

"What is it you need, Milo?"

"I plan to marry Kitty tomorrow at noon, if she shows up," said Milo.

"Oh, she'll be there with boots on. You mark my words. Now, don't you worry 'bout a thing," she said, ushering him back out the door. "You just leave this to me and I'll see ya tomorrow." Milo was barely out the door before Fannie Pearl closed it. He could hear her joyous cry of "Hallelujah" through the door.

He smiled, stepped down off the porch, and made his way to the church. If he was going to get married, he'd best make sure the Pastor was available.

* * *

ABBY RAN INTO THE CAFÉ, startling Lily Jo out of her melancholy. "What's the matter, Abby?"

"Is Kitty here?"

"She's upstairs, why?"

"Can we hang the closed sign for a few minutes? He responded." She whispered.

"What'd he say?"

"He wants to marry her, tomorrow. At noon!"

"Oh my. Flip the sign."

Lily Jo and Abby bounded up the stairs, full of excitement, to find Kitty sitting at the writing desk, staring absently at blank piece of parchment.

"Kitty, there's something I need to tell you," Abby said, taking a seat on the small, blue sofa.

"What's that, Abby?" Kitty asked sadly without bothering to look up.

Abby looked at Lily Jo, who nodded her encouragement, and then back to Kitty, who continued to stare at nothing. Abby remembered when Kitty waited until the last moment to tell her she had accepted a marriage proposal on her behalf, and smiled. She hadn't meant to wait until the last minute to tell Kitty what she'd done, but Milo moved fast.

"You don't need to write that advertisement. You're getting married tomorrow at noon," Abby said.

"Are you kidding me?" She said jumping up from the chair.

Abby smiled, pleased she had Kitty's attention now. "I was looking out for you, like you and Papa did for me. Your wedding is tomorrow at noon. Did Mr. Allen send you with a white rectangle box?"

"Ye-yes, what's the box got to do with this?"

"It's your wedding dress. Papa left one for both of us. I

114

didn't know when I married Samuel because it happened so quick. But I was able to wear it when I married Akecheta."

"*Who* am I supposed to marry tomorrow at noon?" Kitty asked, her eyes wide with panic.

"Oh, I'm sorry, that's the catch. We can't tell you. You have to wait until you get to the altar."

"Why can't you tell me? What if I don't want to marry whoever is there?" Kitty's breathing began to increase, her heart pounding.

"I made a promise, to the groom, but trust me Kitty, you'll want to marry him." Abby smiled.

"Where will we live?" asked Kitty. A million questions forming as the idea of getting married started to sink in, after all she was about to place an advertisement for a husband. Perhaps, Abby's judgement would be better.

"Here," Lily Jo said spreading her arms wide.

"Lily Jo, I cannot marry some stranger and move him into your home," said Kitty.

"No, but you and your stranger can live here and take care of the place for me," Lily Jo said.

"Lily Jo," Abby and Kitty said in unison.

"Why wouldn't you be here, Lily Jo?" asked Abby.

"I—I need a fresh start. There are too many memories here and—and ever since my pa passed, it's as if I've been drowning in them. I don't know if I want to sell the café or not, but I need some time away," she said.

"Where will you go?" asked Kitty.

"I thought I could visit your friend, Shannon, and see if I could serve at Grace Landing for a while. I'd stay with Fannie Pearl until I leave, if you're willing to take over the café for me?"

"What about Kristoff?" Abby asked.

"I have to trust that if he is my future, God will see to it. But, for now, I need to do this for me."

"I understand. I'd be honored to keep the café going, though I doubt I'll be anywhere near as good as you."

"Thank you. Now you have a place to live, a groom, and a wedding dress. Can we see it?"

"I guess so." Kitty stood and walked back to her room to retrieve the special white box. She took it into the room and set it on the table. She'd actually forgotten about the box until now. Carefully, she tore the strings away and opened the box to reveal the loveliest gown she'd ever seen.

"Oh my," Lily Jo gushed.

"You'll be the prettiest bride I've ever seen," said Abby.

"I can't believe you did this. Or that I'm getting married tomorrow." Kitty laughed.

"What are sisters for?" Abby shrugged.

* * *

MILO STOOD at the front of the church with Pastor James, looking out across the pews. Not a single one was empty. If Kitty didn't show, he was going to look like a fool. Everyone assured him she'd be here. Fannie Pearl sure knew how to spread the word, he thought, as his gaze landed on the sweet old lady sitting at the piano.

The church doors opened and Fannie Pearl began to play the Wedding March. The congregation stood as the bride walked in. Milo looked up to see Kitty smiling at him like the vision she was as she walked with Abby down the aisle. They stopped just before him and Pastor James began to speak.

"Who gives this woman to this man?"

"I do," Abby replied and gently laid her sister's hand into Milo's large one. Abby kissed Kitty on the cheek. "Papa would approve," she whispered to Kitty before taking a step back.

"We are gathered here today to celebrate the union of

Milo De Luca and Kathleen Elizabeth O'Byrne as they promise their love and commitment to one another.

"Do you, Milo, take Kitty to be your wedded wife? To love, honor, cherish, and protect for as long as you both shall live?"

"I do, and I also vow to teach you to shoot," said Milo.

"Do you, Kitty, take Milo to be your wedded husband, to love, honor, cherish, and protect for as long as you both shall live?"

"I do, and I promise to *try* not to shoot you again." Kitty smiled.

The congregation erupted in laughter. Pastor James had to yell over them to be heard. "May I present to you, Mr. and Mrs. Milo De Luca. Milo you may kiss your bride."

ABOUT THE AUTHOR

Tonya is from the state of Missouri but has been transplanted in beautiful northern Virginia with her husband, two nearly-grown children, a crazy dog and a wild cat. She has an addiction to pretty journals, coffee, cheesy Hallmark movies - especially around Christmas and is also a diehard country music fan.

With Tonya, it's all about the story, whether she's writing one, reading one, singing one or watching one. The goal is the feeling it evokes and for that reason alone she strives to write stories that allow her readers to experience just that, a feeling.

When Tonya decided to publish she had a bunch of silly thoughts. One, she needed a pen name; a pseudonym. It became a hassle and people were getting confused. SHE was getting confused! She has since seen the error of her ways, but if you see the pseudonym Renea Westlyn - just know it's Tonya. What can I say, she's a bit crazy.

As always, her Grandfather's words continue to push her forward. Sometimes, she simply needs to be reminded of them.

"You should have mailed that letter. It would have brought her great comfort, quit hiding the gift the Lord blessed you with."

Reader Group? Yup, she's got one. Stop in and say Hi! She'd love to get to know you!

Talking with T

PLEASE TAKE A MOMENT TO SHARE YOUR THOUGHTS BY REVIEWING THIS BOOK.

Thank you to all the wonderful readers who take the time to share your thoughts about the books you love. I can't begin to tell you how important you are when it comes to helping other readers and authors alike discover new books!

facebook.com/tonya.r.vanwinkle
twitter.com/TonyaRVanWinkle
instagram.com/tonyavanwinkle
amazon.com/author/tonyavanwinkle
goodreads.com/tonyavanwinkle

The Possum Place and Other Redneck Tales

Wanted: Preacher -Silverpines Series book 9

There are over twenty books in the Silverpines series and several companion novels. You may find them here on the series Amazon page.

Silverpines Series Books

You may also join the Silverpines reader group to learn more and stay up to date with the authors who wrote these books.

Silverpines Reader Group

Each author does have his or her own reader group as well and they all look forward to hearing from you.